Agatha Christie

Cat Among the Pigeons

D0048463

Collins

Collins

HarperCollins Publishers
The News Building
1 London Bridge Street
London SE1 9GF

www.collinselt.com

This *Collins English Readers* edition first published by HarperCollins
Publishers 2012. This second edition published 2017.

10 9 8 7 6 5 4 3 2 1

First published in Great Britain by Collins 1959

www.agathachristie.com

ISBN: 978-0-00-826240-2

Typeset by Davidson Publishing Solutions, Glasgow

Printed and bound by CPI Group (UK) Ltd., Croydon, CR0 4YY

Contents

✦ Introduction ✦

About Collins English Readers

Collins English Readers have been created for readers worldwide whose first language is not English. The stories are carefully graded to ensure that you, the reader, will both enjoy and benefit from your reading experience.

Words which are above the required reading level are underlined the first time they appear in a story. All underlined words are defined in the **Glossary** at the back of the book. Books at levels 1 and 2 take their definitions from the *Collins COBUILD Essential English Dictionary*, and books at levels 3 and above from the *Collins COBUILD Advanced English Dictionary*. Where appropriate, definitions are simplified for level and context.

Alongside the glossary, a **Character list** is provided to help the reader identify who is who, and how they are connected to each other. **Cultural notes** explain historical, cultural and other references. **Maps and diagrams** are provided where appropriate. A **downloadable recording** is also available of the full story. To access the audio, go to www.collinselt.com/eltreadersaudio. The password is the sixth word on page 3 of this book.

To support both teachers and learners, additional materials are available online at www.collinselt.com/readers. These include a **Plot synopsis** and **classroom activities** (both for teachers), **Student activities**, a **level checker** and much more.

About Agatha Christie

Agatha Christie (1890–1976) is known throughout the world as the Queen of Crime. She is the most widely published and translated author of all time and in any language; only the Bible and Shakespeare have sold more copies.

Agatha Christie's first novel was published in 1920. It featured Hercule Poirot, the Belgian detective who has become the most popular detective in crime fiction since Sherlock Holmes.

Collins has published Agatha Christie since 1926.

The Grading Scheme

The Collins COBUILD Grading Scheme has been created using the most up-to-date language usage information available today. Each level is guided by a comprehensive grammar and vocabulary framework, ensuring that the series will perfectly match readers' abilities.

		CEF band	Pages	Word count	Headwords
Level 1	elementary	A2	64	5,000–8,000	approx. 700
Level 2	pre-intermediate	A2–B1	80	8,000–11,000	approx. 900
Level 3	intermediate	B1	96	11,000–20,000	approx. 1,300
Level 4	upper-intermediate	B2	112–128	15,000–26,000	approx. 1,700
Level 5	upper-intermediate+	B2+	128+	22,000–30,000	approx. 2,200
Level 6	advanced	C1	144+	28,000+	2,500+
Level 7	advanced+	C2	160+	*varied*	*varied*

For more information on the Collins COBUILD Grading Scheme go to www.collinselt.com/readers/gradingscheme.

PROLOGUE

SUMMER TERM

It was the first day of the summer term at Meadowbank School for Girls, and Miss Vansittart – one of the teachers – was welcoming the parents and pupils to the beautiful old house. 'How do you do, Mrs Arnold? And, Lydia, did you enjoy your holiday?'

Beside her stood Miss Chadwick – the brilliant Mathematics teacher – who had started Meadowbank school together with Miss Bulstrode, the head teacher. Miss Bulstrode was in her office, where only a few carefully selected people were allowed to go.

Miss Vansittart's words of welcome could be heard all through the school. 'Yes, <u>Lady</u> Garnett, Miss Bulstrode had your letter about the art classes and everything's been arranged.

'How are you, Mrs Bird? Well, I don't think Miss Bulstrode will have time today to discuss that, but you can talk to Miss Rowan.'

◆ ◆ ◆

In a small room on the first floor, Ann Shapland, Miss Bulstrode's secretary, was typing quickly and efficiently. Ann was a nice-looking young woman of thirty-five, with short black hair. She could look very attractive when she wanted to, but at the moment she preferred to look neat and business-<u>like</u> – the perfect secretary to the head teacher of a famous girls' <u>boarding school</u>[1].

From time to time, she looked out of the window to see the new pupils arriving. '<u>My goodness</u>!' said Ann to herself, as an enormous luxury car drove up to the school. A dark-skinned man with a huge beard, wearing long white <u>robes</u>, stepped out of the car, followed by a slim, dark girl.

'That's probably the new princess,' thought Ann. 'I can't imagine her wearing school uniform.' Both Miss Vansittart and Miss Chadwick stepped forward to welcome the important new arrival.

'They'll surely take the princess to see Miss Bulstrode,' decided Ann. 'And I'd better finish typing these letters without making any mistakes.'

Not that Ann often made mistakes. She was a very good secretary, and could choose which jobs she took. In the past she had worked for the head of an oil company, an <u>archaeologist</u> and a government minister. Working at a school was a new experience for her.

She would miss the company of men in this job – though she always had Dennis, who asked her again and again to marry him. She liked him, but it would be very dull to be married to Dennis... It was a shame there weren't any men working at Meadowbank, except a gardener of about eighty.

So Ann was surprised when she looked out of the window and saw a man cutting the hedge – a man who was young, dark and good-looking. 'He must be the new gardener,' said Ann to herself. 'He looks rather interesting...'

She had only one more letter to type. After that she might walk round the garden...

◆ ◆ ◆

Upstairs, Miss Johnson, the <u>matron</u>, was busy sorting out rooms, welcoming new girls, and greeting old pupils. She was pleased it was term time again. She stayed with her married sister in the holidays, but she was really only interested in Meadowbank.

Yes, it was nice that term had started...

◆ ◆ ◆

Mademoiselle Blanche, the new French teacher, was walking on the large grass <u>lawn</u>. She looked with admiration at the strong young man cutting the hedge. '*Très bien*,' she thought, 'very good.'

Mademoiselle Blanche was slim and mouse-like, and noticed everything – though no one really noticed her. She now looked at the cars parked in front of the school. They were all very good cars... Meadowbank must certainly be making lots of money...

◆ ◆ ◆

Miss Eileen Rich, who taught English and Geography, walked quickly towards the school. She had an eager, ugly-looking face and her hair was always untidy. 'I'm here!' she said to herself. 'I'm back at Meadowbank! It seems years since...' As she passed the young gardener she <u>stumbled</u>, and he stopped her from falling, saying, 'Be careful, Miss.'

'Thank you,' said Eileen Rich, without looking at him.

◆ ◆ ◆

Miss Rowan and Miss Blake, the two junior teachers, were walking towards the Sports <u>Pavilion</u>. Miss Rowan was thin and dark, while Miss Blake was <u>plump</u> and fair.

'The new Sports Pavilion looks very impressive,' said Miss Rowan. 'I didn't think it would be ready in time.' Just then the door of the Pavilion opened suddenly, and an athletic young woman with light-red hair came out. She stared at them in an unfriendly way and quickly walked away.

'That must be the new Games teacher[1],' said Miss Blake. 'How rude!'

'She absolutely <u>glared</u> at us,' said Miss Rowan, annoyed.

They both felt a little upset.

◆ ◆ ◆

Miss Bulstrode, the head teacher of Meadowbank, was in her room, which had windows looking out in two directions. One window had a view of the drive and the lawn, and from the other window she could see the large hedge and the path behind the house.

Miss Bulstrode was a tall, impressive woman, with carefully styled grey hair, grey eyes and a firm mouth. It was because of her that Meadowbank was one of the most successful – and expensive – schools in England[2]. Miss Bulstrode accepted different types of pupils, of all ages – girls who didn't fit into other schools, girls who wanted to go to university, girls who only wanted to learn about culture and art, and even foreign royalty. She treated her pupils as individuals, though she also believed in discipline – and she did not accept anyone who was stupid or badly behaved[1].

Miss Bulstrode now greeted the new arrivals. The big man with the beard in white robes said, in very good English, 'I have the honour to bring to you the Princess Shaista.'

Miss Bulstrode wasn't quite sure who the man with the beard was – a secretary, perhaps? – though she knew that her new pupil had just come from a school in Switzerland. Shaista was fashionably dressed and wore a lot of perfume, and although she was only fifteen, she looked older. She had good manners and spoke excellent English.

When Shaista and the secretary had gone, the next people to arrive were Mrs Upjohn and her daughter, Julia. Mrs Upjohn was a pleasant, charming young woman in her late thirties with light hair and freckles. Julia was a plain, freckled child, who looked intelligent and cheerful. As she left the room, Julia said, 'Bye, Mum. Be careful when you light that gas heater, since I won't be there to do it for you.'

Miss Bulstrode turned with a smile to Mrs Upjohn. 'Is there anything you want to tell me about Julia?' she asked.

Mrs Upjohn replied cheerfully, 'Oh no, I don't think so. Julia's a very ordinary child. She's quite healthy and reasonably intelligent. She's very excited about coming to school here.' She moved to the window and looked out. 'How lovely and tidy your garden is. It's so hard to find a real gardener now. I sometimes think— Well!' exclaimed Mrs Upjohn, still looking out of the window – 'how extraordinary!'

But Miss Bulstrode was not listening, because out of the other window she had just seen Lady Veronica Carlton stumbling along the path, talking to herself and clearly very drunk indeed.

This had happened before. Lady Veronica was a charming woman, except when she was drunk. She was usually looked after by her cousin, but today it seemed that she had escaped. Her twin daughters had arrived by train earlier, but no one had expected Lady Veronica.

Mrs Upjohn was still talking, but Miss Bulstrode, who saw that Lady Veronica would soon start shouting and behaving badly, wasn't listening. Just as Miss Bulstrode was planning what to do, she saw Miss Chadwick appear, slightly out of breath.

'It's disgraceful,' said Lady Veronica very loudly to Miss Chadwick. 'They didn't want me to come here. I'm going to take the girls home – I love them and I want them at home—'

'That's excellent, Lady Veronica,' said Miss Chadwick. 'We're so pleased you're here.' She gently led Lady Veronica away from the house. 'I particularly want you to see the new Sports Pavilion. You'll love it.' Their voices became quieter as they walked away.

Miss Bulstrode watched with relief – she could always rely on her dear Chaddy! – and then turned back to Mrs Upjohn, who had been talking for some time…

'… though, of course,' Mrs Upjohn was saying, 'my work in the war wasn't very exciting – not jumping out of a plane, or sabotage. I worked in an office most of the time. But sometimes it was quite funny – all the secret agents in Geneva knew each other, and often went to the same bar.'

Mrs Upjohn stopped suddenly with a smile. 'I'm sorry. I've been talking too much, and you have so many other people to see.' She shook Miss Bulstrode's hand, said goodbye and left.

Miss Bulstrode frowned. She had a feeling that she had missed something important. But she didn't worry about it for long. This was the first day of summer term, and her school was a great success. Miss Bulstrode had no idea that in a few weeks Meadowbank would be the scene of confusion and murder…

Chapter 1

Revolution in Ramat

About two months earlier, certain events took place that would greatly affect the famous girls' school.

In the Palace of Ramat, two young men sat smoking. One man was dark, with large, sad-looking eyes. He was Prince Ali Yusuf, the <u>Sheikh</u> of Ramat, a small but very rich country in the Middle East. The other young man, Bob Rawlinson, had light hair and freckles, and was the prince's private pilot. The two men had been at school together and were very close friends.

'They shot at us, Bob,' said Prince Ali, unable to believe it. 'They wanted to shoot down our plane.'

'Yes, they did,' said Bob <u>grimly</u>. 'You should have left the country two weeks ago, Ali. Now it's too late. Perhaps you can go to the British Embassy – shall I talk to my friend who works there?'[3]

Ali Yusuf's face went red with anger. 'I will never hide in your Embassy! The rebels would probably drag me from the building.' He sighed. 'I don't understand,' he said sadly. 'My grandfather was a cruel man, who killed his enemies without pity. And yet he is still admired and respected! And I? I have built hospitals, schools and houses… all the things people want. So why are they rebelling against me?'

Bob Rawlinson sighed. 'Let's not talk about that now. The most important thing is to get you safely out of the country. Is there anybody in the Army you can trust?'

Slowly, Prince Ali Yusuf shook his head. 'I do not know,' he said. 'I cannot be sure – there are secret agents everywhere. They hear everything – they know everything.'

'Even at the <u>airstrip</u>—' Bob stopped. 'But we can trust Achmed. He caught someone trying to sabotage the plane – someone we thought we could trust. So, if you want to leave the country, Ali, we must go soon.'

'I know – I know. I am quite certain now that if I stay I will be killed.' Ali spoke without emotion – as if his future was only of slight interest to him.

'We may be killed anyway,' Bob warned him. 'We'll have to fly north over the mountains. At this time of year it's very dangerous.'

Ali Yusuf looked worried. 'I don't want anything to happen to you, Bob.'

'Don't worry about me, Ali. I'm not important. No – it's you – I don't want to make you leave. If some people in the Army are loyal—'

'I don't want to run away,' said Ali simply. 'But nor do I want to be killed by a crowd of angry people.' After a moment's thought he made his decision. 'Very well,' he said with a sigh. 'We will try to leave. When?'

'This afternoon,' said Bob. 'Go and inspect that new road, and stop at the airstrip. I'll have the plane ready to go. We can't take anything with us.'

'There is only one thing I wish to take with me,' said Ali Yusuf. He took out a small leather bag from under his shirt, and poured its contents on the table.

Bob held his breath for a moment. Before him was a pile of beautiful precious jewels. 'My goodness! Are they real?'

Ali looked amused. 'Of course they are real. They are worth about a million pounds.'

'A million pounds!' Bob picked up the jewels and let them fall through his fingers. 'It's fantastic. Like a <u>fairy story</u>.'

'Yes.' The dark young man nodded. 'Such jewels have a strange effect on people – death and violence follow them around. And women – beautiful jewels make women go mad. I would not trust any woman with these jewels. But I will trust you.'

'Me?' Bob stared.

'Yes,' replied his friend. 'I do not want these jewels to be taken by my enemies. I do not know when the <u>rebellion</u> will take place, but I may not live to reach the airstrip this afternoon. Take the jewels and do the best you can.'

'But I don't understand,' said Bob. 'What do you want me to do with them?'

'Take them out of the country somehow,' Ali said calmly. 'You will think of a plan.'

'But Ali, I don't know how to do that.'

Ali sat back in his chair and smiled. 'You are sensible, Bob, and you are honest. When we were at school, you always had clever ideas. I will give you the name and address of a man who deals with such things for me – in case I do not survive. Do not look so worried, Bob. Do the best you can, that is all I ask. I shall not blame you if you fail. It is <u>as Allah wills</u>.'

'You're crazy!' exclaimed Bob.

'No. I believe in fate, that is all.'

'But Ali – a million pounds. Aren't you afraid that I'll keep the jewels for myself?'

Ali Yusuf smiled at his friend. 'No, Bob,' he said, 'I am not afraid of that.'

CHAPTER 2

THE WOMAN ON THE BALCONY

Bob Rawlinson was very unhappy as he walked along the crowded main street outside the palace. He felt that everyone knew he was carrying a million pounds in his pocket. As he walked along he tried to think. Where was he going? What was he planning to do? He had no idea, and not much time.

He went into a local café and ordered some lemon tea. As he drank it, he slowly began to feel better. The atmosphere of the café was calming. At a nearby table, an elderly Arab was peacefully sitting and drinking his hot tea, and behind him two men played a game of <u>dice</u>. It was a good place to sit and think.

And he *had* to think. He'd been given jewels worth a million pounds, and he had to get them out of the country as soon as possible. What was he going to do? He couldn't involve his friend at the British Embassy. What he needed was an ordinary person who was leaving the country – a businessman or a tourist would be best.

Then suddenly Bob thought of his sister, Joan Sutcliffe – of course! Joan had been in Ramat for two months with her daughter Jennifer, who was recovering from an illness. They were going back to England by ship in a few days' time.

Joan was the ideal person, Bob thought. Yes, he could trust Joan, even with jewels.

But wait a minute… could he really trust Joan? Joan was honest, yes, but she would talk – talk about the jewels. It would be safer if she didn't know what she was carrying.

Bob looked at his watch, stood up and left the café. Outside everything seemed so normal – there was nothing to show that rebels were planning a revolution.

Bob walked to Ramat's leading hotel. The hotel clerk behind the desk knew Bob well and smiled at him. 'Good morning, sir. Do you want your sister? I'm afraid she and your niece have gone to visit the temple.'

Bob swore quietly to himself – Joan wouldn't be home for hours. 'I'll go up to her room,' he said, and the clerk gave him the key.

Inside his sister's room it was very untidy. Golf clubs lay across a chair and tennis racquets had been thrown on the bed. Clothes were lying around, and the table was covered with rolls of film, postcards, books and souvenirs.

Bob now had a problem. He wouldn't see Joan before he flew Ali out that afternoon, and he couldn't just leave her a package of jewels and a note, because he'd probably been watched and followed to the hotel. He hadn't noticed anyone – but that just meant they were good at their job. There was nothing suspicious in coming to see his sister, but if he left her a package and a note, the package would be opened and the note would be read.

If only he had more time!

He looked around the room… and then he had an idea. With a smile, he took from his pocket the little tool kit he always carried. He saw that his niece Jennifer had some <u>plasticine</u> – that would help.

He worked quickly. Once, he looked up at the open window – he felt that someone was watching him. But no, there was no balcony outside this room.

When he finished, he nodded in approval. He was sure that nobody – not even Joan or Jennifer – would notice what he'd done. When he had cleared up he wrote an ordinary note to his sister. He would leave a message with someone else to give to Joan in England. He wrote quickly:

Dear Joan – I came to ask if you'd like to play golf this evening, but if you've been to the temple, you'll probably be too tired. What about tomorrow? Five o'clock at the Club.

Yours, Bob

Next he telephoned the British Embassy, and was connected to his friend, John Edmundson. 'John? It's Bob Rawlinson. Can you meet me somewhere when you finish work? Or earlier, if you can – it's important. Well, actually, it's about a girl...' He gave an embarrassed cough. 'She's wonderful, really wonderful – but it's a bit difficult.'

Because all the telephones in Ramat were <u>tapped</u> and listened to, Bob and John Edmundson had their own secret code. A 'wonderful girl' meant something urgent and important[3].

'Really, Bob, you and your girls!' said Edmundson with <u>disapproval</u>. 'All right, I'll meet you at two o'clock.' Bob heard a 'click' as the person who had been listening to their conversation put down the phone.

He would meet Edmundson outside the main bank at two o'clock and tell him about the secret hiding place. Joan and Jennifer were travelling on a slow boat back to England, which would take six weeks. By that time the revolution in Ramat would have either succeeded or failed, and Ali Yusuf might be safely in Europe – or they might both be dead.

Bob looked carefully around the room before he left. It looked exactly the same – peaceful and untidy. His <u>harmless</u> note to Joan was on the table. There was no one in the corridor when Bob left the room.

♦ ◆ ♦

The woman in the room next door to Joan Sutcliffe's stepped back from the balcony. There was a mirror in her hand.

She had gone out on the balcony to look at her face closely in the clear sunlight. Then she saw something else. She was holding her mirror so that it reflected the mirror of the wardrobe in the room next to hers – and in the wardrobe mirror she saw a man doing something very strange and unexpected.

She stood still, watching the man. He could not see her from where he was, and she could only see him because of the double reflection in the two mirrors.

Once, the man did look up suddenly towards the window, but since there was no one there, he lowered his head again. When he had finished what he was doing he wrote a note, which he left on the table. Then the woman heard him make a telephone call, and though she didn't hear the words, he sounded cheerful and relaxed. Then she heard the door close.

The woman waited a few minutes and then opened her door. The door of the next room was locked, but she opened the lock quickly and expertly with a small knife.

She went in, closing the door behind her, and picked up and read the note. Just as she put the note down, she heard voices and ran to the window.

Below, Joan Sutcliffe was complaining in a loud voice to a young man from the British Embassy. 'Leave Ramat now? I never heard such nonsense! Everything's perfectly quiet here.' Her daughter Jennifer, a pale girl of fifteen, stood next to her.

'We're going home by boat in a few days anyway,' continued Mrs Sutcliffe. 'The doctor said that travelling by sea will be good for Jennifer's health. I refuse to change my plans and fly back to England in this silly hurry.'

'You don't have to fly to England,' said the young man <u>persuasively</u>. 'You can both fly out of Ramat and get on your boat at the next port.'

'With all our luggage?' asked Joan Sutcliffe. 'We have a lot of luggage.'

'Yes, yes, I can arrange that. I've got a big car waiting outside. We can load everything and leave right away.'

'Oh, very well,' said Mrs Sutcliffe. 'I suppose we'd better pack.'

'At once, if you don't mind.'

The woman in the bedroom stepped away from the window. She looked at the address on one of the luggage labels, and then went quickly back to her own room.

A few moments later Joan Sutcliffe arrived at the door of her room, followed by the hotel clerk. 'Your brother went up to your room, Mrs Sutcliffe,' he said. 'But I think you have just missed him.'

'How annoying,' said Mrs Sutcliffe and thanked the clerk. 'I suppose Bob's <u>fussing</u> too,' she said to Jennifer. 'I can't see any sign of a revolution in the streets myself. This door's unlocked. How careless people are.'

'Perhaps it was Uncle Bob,' said Jennifer.

'I wish I'd seen him… Oh, he's left me a note.' She read it quickly.

'Bob isn't worried,' she said. 'He obviously doesn't know anything about a revolution – it's all a big fuss about nothing. I hate packing when it's so hot. Come on, Jennifer, get your things ready quickly.'

'I've never been in a revolution,' said Jennifer thoughtfully.

'And you won't be in one now,' said her mother <u>sharply</u>. 'Nothing will happen.'

Jennifer looked disappointed.

CHAPTER 3

INTRODUCING MR ROBINSON

Six weeks later a young man entered a small office in London. Behind a desk sat <u>Colonel</u> Pikeaway, a fat, middle-aged man wearing an untidy suit. The Colonel always looked half asleep, and he smoked a lot of cigars.

'Oh,' said Colonel Pikeaway, as the young man entered. 'Your name's Edmundson, isn't it? You were at the British Embassy in Ramat at the time of the revolution.'

'That's right, sir,' said the young man. 'John Edmundson. They said you – er – wanted to see me.'

'Sit down,' said Colonel Pikeaway. 'You were a friend of Bob Rawlinson's, weren't you?'

'I knew him fairly well, yes,' said Edmundson.

'So you know he's dead, then,' said Colonel Pikeaway. 'Bob Rawlinson flew Ali Yusuf out of Ramat on the day of the revolution. The plane crashed into a mountain and the <u>wreckage</u> has only just been found – with two bodies.'

He paused and looked at Edmundson. 'Some people – very important people – have asked us to investigate this case,' he continued. 'You've heard, perhaps, that nothing valuable was found on the bodies, or in the wreckage. We know that Bob Rawlinson and Ali Yusuf were great friends. Did Rawlinson say anything to you before he flew out of Ramat?'

'I think Bob did want to tell me something important, sir,' said Edmundson cautiously. 'We knew that all the telephones in Ramat were tapped, so Bob and I used a simple code about a "wonderful girl". Bob rang me and used the code on the day the revolution started. I arranged to meet him outside the main bank, but I never got there because there was fighting and the police closed the road. Bob flew Prince Ali out the same afternoon.'

'I see,' said Pikeaway, and thought for a moment. 'Do you know Mrs Sutcliffe?'

'Bob Rawlinson's sister?' said Edmundson. 'Yes, I did meet her and her daughter in Ramat. She was much older than Bob.'

'Mrs Sutcliffe and her daughter arrive back in England tomorrow. Do you think that Bob Rawlinson would have told his sister an important secret?'

'It's difficult to say – but no, I don't think so.'

Colonel Pikeaway sighed and was silent for a moment, before he said goodbye to Edmundson. 'Thank you for coming.'

'I'm sorry I haven't been able to help, sir.'

When John Edmundson left, Colonel Pikeaway picked up the phone. 'Send Agent R in to see me,' he said. 'I've got a job for him.'

◆ ◆ ◆

Colonel Pikeaway looked up as a good-looking young man – tall, dark and <u>muscular</u> – entered the room. The Colonel gave a broad smile. 'I'm sending you to a girls' school,' he said. 'To Meadowbank.'

'Meadowbank!' said the young man in surprise. 'Are the girls making bombs in Chemistry class?'

'Don't ask silly questions,' said the Colonel, 'and listen. I'm sure you've heard about the recent death of Prince Ali Yusuf of Ramat. His closest living relative is his cousin, Princess Shaista, who starts at Meadowbank in the summer term. I want you to watch her closely and report to me if anyone seems interested in her.'

The young man nodded. 'And what will I be doing, teaching?'

'All the teachers there are women.' Colonel Pikeaway looked at him thoughtfully. 'No, you're going to be the gardener. Good gardeners are hard to find at the moment, and I know you have a lot of experience. I'll write you some good references to make sure they give you a job. And you need to hurry – summer term starts soon.'

'So I do the gardening and keep my eyes open, is that right?'

'That's right,' said the Colonel. He started writing. 'Your new name is Adam Goodman. Go and invent a new past history for yourself and then get to Meadowbank as soon as possible.' He looked at his watch. 'I'm expecting Mr Robinson now.'

A <u>buzzer</u> went on the Colonel's desk. 'There he is now. Mr Robinson is always on time.'

'Tell me,' said Adam curiously. 'Who is he really? What's his real name?'

'His name,' said Colonel Pikeaway, 'is Mr Robinson. That's all I know, and that's all anybody knows.'[3]

◆ ◆ ◆

Mr Robinson was fat and well dressed, with a yellow face, sad dark eyes, and large, very white teeth. He and Colonel Pikeaway greeted each other politely. 'It's very good of you to help us,' said the Colonel.

'I hear things, you know,' said Mr Robinson. 'I know a lot of people, and they tell me things.'

'Did you know that Prince Ali Yusuf's plane has been found?' asked Colonel Pikeaway.

'Yes,' said Mr Robinson. 'And I can tell you that it wasn't Bob Rawlinson's fault the plane crashed. The plane was sabotaged by a man called Achmed, the senior mechanic. Rawlinson trusted him, but Achmed now has a well-paid job with the new Ramat government.'

'So it *was* sabotage! We didn't know that for sure.'

'And now we know that Prince Ali Yusuf is dead,' continued Mr Robinson, 'we would like to find the package he left behind – the jewels.'

'They weren't found on Ali Yusuf's body, as far as we know.'

'No, because he gave them to Bob Rawlinson.'

'Are you sure of that?' asked Pikeaway sharply. 'They weren't on young Rawlinson's body, either.'

'In that case,' said Mr Robinson, 'Rawlinson must have got them out of the country some other way.'

'Have you any idea how?' asked Pikeaway.

'Rawlinson went up to his sister's hotel room to write her a note and stayed there for about twenty minutes. He could have written his note in three minutes. What did he do the rest of the time?'

'So you think that he hid the jewels in his sister's luggage?'

'It seems likely, does it not?' agreed Mr Robinson. 'Mrs Sutcliffe and her daughter left Ramat that same day, and they arrive back in England by boat tomorrow, I believe.'

Pikeaway nodded. 'We've arranged to look after them,' he said.

'If she has the jewels, she will be in danger.' Mr Robinson closed his eyes. 'There are other people interested in them.'

Colonel Pikeaway asked carefully, 'And what is your – er – interest in the jewels?'

'I represent a certain group of people,' said Mr Robinson. 'Prince Ali Yusuf bought some of the jewels from us, and so we are interested in finding the jewels now. I'm sure the prince would have approved. I will not say any more – these matters are private.' He paused. 'Do you know who was staying in the hotel rooms on either side of Mrs Sutcliffe's room?'

'On the left hand side was Señora Angelica de Toredo,' said Colonel Pikeaway. 'She's a Spanish – er – dancer – though I don't think she was Spanish, or a very good dancer. On the other side was a schoolteacher, I believe.'

Mr Robinson smiled. 'You always know everything,' he said. 'I hope that – together – we know enough...'

CHAPTER 4

RETURN OF A TRAVELLER

'Oh dear!' said Mrs Sutcliffe, as she looked out of her hotel window. 'It's always raining in England.'

'It's lovely to be back,' said Jennifer. 'I love hearing everyone speak English in the streets, and I'm looking forward to having a really good afternoon tea, with lots of cakes.'

'Now let me make sure we have all our luggage,' said her mother. 'People are so dishonest these days. I'm sure that man on the boat was trying to steal my green bag. And there was another man on the train…' Mrs Sutcliffe counted. 'Yes – yes, that's all right. All fourteen pieces of luggage are here.'

'Can we have tea now?' said Jennifer. 'I'm very hungry.'

'All right, but I really need to rest, so you must go down by yourself. I don't know why your father couldn't leave work and meet us, especially as he hasn't seen us for three months.' She gave Jennifer some money for tea and watched her daughter leave the room.

After a few minutes there was a knock at the door. It was a young man in a dark blue uniform, carrying a tool bag. 'Electrician,' he said. 'I've come to repair the lights in the bathroom.'

Mrs Sutcliffe had just shown the electrician the bathroom when the telephone rang. 'Hello… Yes, Mrs Sutcliffe speaking.'

'My name is Derek O'Connor – I work for the government. Can I come up to your room, Mrs Sutcliffe? It's about your brother.'

'Bob? Do you have any news?'

'I'm afraid so – yes.'

'Oh… Oh, I see… Yes, come up. My room's on the third floor, number 310.' Mrs Sutcliffe sat down on the bed. She knew what the news must be.

Soon there was a knock on the door and Mrs Sutcliffe let in another young man. 'Please tell me,' said Mrs Sutcliffe. 'Bob's dead, isn't he?'

'Yes, Mrs Sutcliffe, I'm afraid so,' said O'Connor. 'Your brother was flying Prince Ali Yusuf out from Ramat and they crashed in the mountains. There was no definite news until a few days ago, but now the wreckage of the plane has been found. He and Prince Ali must have died immediately.'

'I'm not at all surprised,' said Mrs Sutcliffe. Her voice shook a little but she was in control of herself. 'I knew Bob would die young. He was always doing such dangerous things.' A tear fell down her cheek. 'It's such a shock.'

'I know – I'm very sorry.'

'Thank you for coming to tell me,' Mrs Sutcliffe said.

'There's something I have to ask you,' said O'Connor. 'Did your brother give you anything – a package – to bring back to England?'

She shook her head. 'No. Why do you think that?'

'Your brother had a rather important package, and we don't know where it is. He came to your hotel the day the revolution started.'

'I know,' said Mrs Sutcliffe. 'But all he left me was a note asking me to play golf the next day.' Another tear fell down her cheek. 'Oh dear, I need a handkerchief. Where's my bag? Perhaps I left it in the other room.'

'I'll get it for you,' said O'Connor.

He went through the bedroom door and stopped as he saw a young man bending over a suitcase. 'Electrician,' said the young man quickly. 'There's something wrong with the lights.'

O'Connor pressed the light switch. 'They seem all right to me,' he said pleasantly.

'I must be in the wrong room,' said the electrician. He quickly picked up his tool bag and left.

O'Connor frowned as he took Mrs Sutcliffe's bag back to her. 'Excuse me,' he said, and picked up the phone. 'Room 310 here. Have you just sent up an electrician?' He waited. 'No? No, I thought you hadn't. No, there's nothing wrong.'

He put down the phone and turned to Mrs Sutcliffe. 'The office didn't send up an electrician,' he told her. 'I think that man was a thief.'

Mrs Sutcliffe looked quickly in her bag. 'He hasn't taken anything. I still have all my money.'

'If your brother didn't give you a package,' said O'Connor, 'he might have hidden it in your luggage instead.'

'But why would Bob do such a thing?' asked Mrs Sutcliffe. 'It sounds very unlikely.'

'Would you mind if we searched your luggage now?' asked O'Connor. 'It might be very important. I can help,' he added persuasively. 'I'm very good at packing.'

'Oh well,' said Mrs Sutcliffe, 'I suppose so – if it's really important…'

◆ ◆ ◆

'Mummy, why have you been unpacking?' Jennifer asked in surprise when she returned.

'Don't ask *me* why,' said her mother. 'It's possible that your Uncle Bob put something in my luggage to bring home. He didn't give you anything, Jennifer, did he?'

'No, he didn't,' said Jennifer. 'Have you been unpacking my things, too?'

'We've unpacked everything,' said Derek O'Connor cheerfully, 'and we haven't found anything. Can I order you a drink, Mrs Sutcliffe, while I pack up again?'

'I wouldn't mind a cup of tea,' said Mrs Sutcliffe.

O'Connor ordered the tea, then packed up Mrs Sutcliffe's things again quickly and neatly.

'There's just one thing more, Mrs Sutcliffe,' he said. 'I'd like you to be very careful. Are you staying in London long?'

'We're going back home to the country tomorrow, with my husband.'

'That's all right then. But if anything strange happens, call the police straight away.'

◆ ◆ ◆

From a local newspaper:

A man named Andrew Ball appeared in court yesterday, charged with breaking into the house of Mr Henry Sutcliffe. Police arrested him as he tried to escape from the house, and nothing was taken. Ball admitted that he was guilty of trying to steal, saying that he had no work and was looking for money.

◆ ◆ ◆

'I told you to have the lock on that side door repaired,' said Mr Sutcliffe to his wife.

'My dear Henry,' said Mrs Sutcliffe, 'I've been abroad for the last three months. And burglars can always find a way in if they really want to.'

'I don't understand,' said Jennifer. 'How did the police know the house was being burgled and get here in time to catch him?'

'It seems extraordinary that he didn't take anything,' commented her mother.

'Are you quite sure nothing's missing, Joan?' demanded her husband.

Mrs Sutcliffe sighed. 'It's very hard to know,' she said. 'There was such a mess in my bedroom.'

'Can I have some more pudding?' asked Jennifer.

'I suppose so,' said her mother, 'though I do hope they won't think you're too greedy at school. Meadowbank isn't an ordinary school, remember.'

'I don't think I really want to go to Meadowbank,' said Jennifer. 'I know a girl whose cousin said it was awful.'

'That's enough, Jennifer,' said Mrs Sutcliffe. 'You're very lucky to be going to Meadowbank. It's a very good school.'

◆ ◆ ◆

When Andrew Ball had been sent to prison for three months, Derek O'Connor rang Colonel Pikeaway. 'We let Ball have plenty of time to search the house before we arrested him,' he told the Colonel, 'in case he knew where the jewels were. But he didn't find anything.'

'And neither did you,' replied Colonel Pikeaway. 'Perhaps we're wrong, and Rawlinson didn't hide the jewels in his sister's luggage.'

'Are there any other possibilities?' asked O'Connor.

'Oh, yes,' said the Colonel. 'They may still be in Ramat, hidden in the hotel or near the airstrip. Or maybe Mrs Sutcliffe had the package of jewels without knowing, and threw them into the sea on her way home.

'And that,' he added thoughtfully, 'might be the best place for them.'

CHAPTER 5

LETTERS FROM MEADOWBANK SCHOOL

Letter from Julia Upjohn to her mother:

Dear Mummy,

I've <u>settled in</u> now and I like it here very much. There's another new girl called Jennifer and she and I do things together. We both like tennis, and Jennifer is rather good. She was in Ramat when that revolution started, but she missed it because they were taken away by someone from the Embassy.

I like Miss Bulstrode, but she can be frightening. I've heard that she's going to retire soon and that Miss Vansittart will be the new head teacher, but I'm sure it isn't true. Miss Rich, our English teacher, is wonderful. When she reads Shakespeare it all seems different and real. Someone told me she wasn't here last term. We do French with Mademoiselle Blanche, who seems to be bored a lot of the time. Our Games teacher, Miss Springer, is awful. She's got red hair and smells when she's hot.

There are a lot of foreign girls here, and a princess who says she was going to marry Prince Ali Yusuf if he hadn't been killed in that plane crash. Jennifer says that isn't true, and that Prince Ali liked someone else. Jennifer knows a lot of interesting things.

I know you're leaving on your trip soon. Don't forget your passport like you did last time!

Love from Julia

◆ ◆ ◆

Letter from Jennifer Sutcliffe to her mother:

Dear Mummy,

It really isn't bad here, and I'm enjoying it more than I expected. The weather has been very fine. Do you think I could have a new tennis racquet? Mine feels all wrong. And can I start to learn Greek? I love languages. Some of us are going to London to the theatre next week. The food here is very good. Yesterday we had chicken, and lovely cakes for tea.

Your loving daughter,

Jennifer

Letter from Ann Shapland to Dennis Rathbone:

Dear Dennis,

I'd love to have dinner with you, but I don't have any free time until the weekend of the third week of term. I'll let you know.

It's rather fun working in a school. But I'm glad I'm not a teacher – I'd go mad!

Yours ever,

Ann

Letter from Miss Johnson to her sister:

Dear Edith,

Everything here is much the same as usual. The summer term is always nice. The garden is looking beautiful and we've got a new gardener to help old Briggs – he's young, strong and good-looking, which is a pity. Girls are so silly.

Miss Bulstrode hasn't said anything more about retiring, so I hope she's changed her mind. If Miss Vansittart became head teacher I really think I'd have to leave.

Give my love to Richard and the children.

Elspeth

Letter from Miss Vansittart to a friend:

Dear Gloria,

The summer term has started, and all the new girls are settling in well. But the new Games teacher, Miss Springer, is not a success and the girls don't like her. She is also rather rude and very <u>nosey</u>, and asks far too many personal questions. Mademoiselle Blanche, the new French teacher, is quite nice but is not a very good teacher.

Miss Bulstrode has not yet talked to me about the future, but I think she has decided what to do. I will be proud to carry on her fine work at Meadowbank.

Yours ever,

Eleanor

Letter from Adam Goodman to Colonel Pikeaway, sent in the usual way:

Princess Shaista arrived in a huge luxury car. I hardly recognized her the next day in her school uniform. I am already on friendly terms with her, and she was asking me about the flowers until the Games teacher, Miss Springer, took her away and told me not to talk to pupils. An old teacher called Miss Chadwick keeps an eye on me, so I'm being careful.

No sign, so far, of anything strange — but I hope something will happen soon.

CHAPTER 6

EARLY DAYS

The teachers were all talking together – discussing their holidays, the Sports Pavilion and the new girls. Then attention turned to the new teachers. Mademoiselle Blanche answered some polite questions about France, and Miss Springer began to talk about herself.

Miss Springer had a high opinion of herself. She talked loudly about how much she had been valued at other schools, and how her colleagues and head teachers had welcomed her advice. 'Though of course some people weren't grateful and refused to face the truth,' she said. 'I'm not like that. And I'm good at finding things out. Several times I've discovered a nasty scandal and told everyone about it. You shouldn't teach in a school if you have something to hide.' She laughed loudly. 'You'd be surprised if I told you some of the things I've found out about people. But I was just doing my duty.'

Miss Springer laughed again. She didn't notice that nobody else was amused.

◆ ◆ ◆

Miss Bulstrode was trying not to smile as Miss Johnson complained to Shaista about the way she was dressed. 'You are dressed like a woman, not a girl. That top is too tight.'

'But I want to look like a woman,' explained Shaista helpfully.

'You're only fifteen,' said Miss Johnson.

'Fifteen – that is a woman!' said Shaista. 'And I look like a woman, do I not?'

Miss Bulstrode nodded seriously. 'I understand your point of view, Shaista,' she said, 'but I suggest that you wear these clothes when you go to London or to a party, not every day.'

When Shaista had gone, Miss Bulstrode smiled at Miss Johnson. 'It's true – Shaista does look fully grown up. <u>Physically</u> she's totally different to Julia Upjohn, for example. It's good to have a school full of girls who are different.'

Miss Bulstrode went back to correcting homework, and thought about her school. She had worked hard and taken risks to make Meadowbank a success. And Miss Chadwick had always been there to help her. Now Miss Bulstrode had decided to retire while she was still successful. She didn't know what Miss Chadwick would do – perhaps she would prefer to carry on teaching.

Miss Bulstrode rang for Ann Shapland and began to dictate letters. Ann was a very good secretary, thought Miss Bulstrode. Better than the one before, who had left so suddenly.

When the letters were done, Miss Bulstrode sighed with relief. 'Writing to parents is very dull,' she said to Ann. 'Tell me, why did you become a secretary?'

'I don't really know,' said Ann. 'It just happened. But I've had lots of interesting jobs. And I can't stay in one job for very long because of my mother – I have to go and look after her at times. I like change – it's never dull.'

'My job – teaching – is never dull,' said Miss Bulstrode. 'I'll miss it when I retire.'

'Are you going to retire?' asked Ann in surprise. 'Why?'

'Because I've done all I can for Meadowbank – it's someone else's turn.'

'Miss Vansittart, I suppose?' said Ann. 'She'll carry on your work.'

But is that what I want? thought Miss Bulstrode as Ann left the room to start typing. Do I want Eleanor Vansittart just to carry on my work? Or do I want someone with personality – like Eileen Rich – to bring new and fresh ideas to Meadowbank?

She looked up as Miss Chadwick came in. 'What's wrong, Chaddy?'

'Nothing,' said Miss Chadwick with a frown. 'Nothing really. I just have a feeling that something isn't quite right – but I don't know why. And I don't like Mademoiselle Blanche very much, or Miss Springer.'

'Having new teachers is always upsetting,' said Miss Bulstrode.

'Yes,' agreed Miss Chadwick. 'That must be it. And we must keep an eye on that new gardener. It's a pity he's so young and good-looking.'

Both women nodded. They knew what damage a good-looking young man could do to the hearts of teenage girls.

Chapter 7

<u>Straws</u> in the Wind[4]

'Were you talking to one of the young ladies just now?' Briggs asked his new gardener.

'Just for a few minutes,' said Adam <u>sulkily</u>. 'I didn't say anything wrong.'

'I don't say you did, boy. But you'd better be careful,' Briggs told him. 'All these girls together with no men to distract them. Miss Bulstrode wouldn't like it. Ah, here she comes now.'

Miss Bulstrode was approaching. 'Good morning,' she said. 'I'd like one of you to repair the wire netting round the tennis court. As soon as possible.' She walked off again.

'She just comes along – giving orders,' said Briggs, annoyed. 'But I suppose you should go and repair that netting when you've finished here.'

'Oh, all right,' said Adam, still sounding sulky.

As she walked back to the school, Miss Bulstrode met Miss Vansittart coming in the opposite direction.

'What a hot afternoon,' said Miss Vansittart.

'Yes, it is,' agreed Miss Bulstrode. Then she frowned. 'Have you noticed that young man – the young gardener? He's very good-looking. The girls notice him. We'll have to keep an eye on them.' She laughed. 'There's never a dull moment running a school. Do you ever find life dull here, Eleanor?'

'No indeed,' said Miss Vansittart. 'I find the work here very exciting and satisfying. You must feel very proud of the great success you've achieved.'

'Tell me, Eleanor,' said Miss Bulstrode, 'if you were running the school instead of me, what changes would you make?'

'I don't think I would change anything,' said Eleanor Vansittart. 'I think Meadowbank is perfect the way it is.'

Now was the time, thought Miss Bulstrode, to ask Eleanor Vansittart to be the next head teacher[1]. But something was stopping her...

A bell sounded in the distance.

'It's time for my German class,' said Miss Vansittart. 'I must go.' She hurried towards the school, and Miss Bulstrode followed her slowly – and almost bumped into Eileen Rich, hurrying from a side path.

'Oh, I'm sorry,' said Eileen Rich, 'I didn't see you. I was going to my English class.' Her hair, as usual, was very untidy.

'You enjoy teaching, don't you?' said Miss Bulstrode. 'Why exactly do you like it?'

Eileen Rich ran a hand through her hair and thought for a moment. 'Because you don't know what you're going to get,' she said, 'or how the girls will answer. It's so incredibly exciting.'

Miss Bulstrode nodded in agreement. 'And do you have your own ideas about running a school?' she asked.

'Oh yes,' replied Eileen Rich. 'I'm sure some of them wouldn't work, but you have to take risks in life, don't you, if you feel strongly enough about something?'

'So you don't mind leading a dangerous life,' smiled Miss Bulstrode.

A dark look passed over Eileen Rich's face. 'I suppose not,' she said. 'I must go now. The girls will be waiting.' She hurried off.

Miss Bulstrode was still watching her walk away when Miss Chadwick came to find her.

'You look worried, Honoria,' said Miss Chadwick.

'Yes, I am worried – I can't decide what to do,' said Miss Bulstrode.

'Are you still thinking about retiring? You really shouldn't. Meadowbank needs you.'

'You love Meadowbank, don't you, Chaddy?'

'It's the best school in England,' said Miss Chadwick. 'We can be proud of ourselves for starting it.'

◆ ◆ ◆

'I can't play with this tennis racquet,' said Jennifer, throwing it down in despair. 'It's been <u>restrung</u> but the balance is all wrong.'

'It's much better than mine,' said Julia, comparing the two racquets. 'The strings on mine are really loose.'

'I'd still rather have your racquet,' said Jennifer, picking it up and swinging it.

'Well, I'd rather have yours,' said Julia. 'Shall we <u>swap</u>?'

'All right then,' Jennifer agreed, and the two girls took off their name labels and put them on each other's racquet.

◆ ◆ ◆

Adam was mending the netting round the tennis court when the door of the Sports Pavilion opened and Mademoiselle Blanche, the little mouse-like French teacher, looked out. She seemed surprised to see Adam, and went back inside, with a guilty look that made Adam immediately suspicious.

Soon Mademoiselle Blanche came out again and closed the door. 'It is a very fine Sports Pavilion,' she said to Adam as she passed. 'Today is the first time I have been inside. I wish to write home to my friends in France who keep a school.'

Adam was curious. Mademoiselle Blanche could go anywhere in the school that she liked. Why was she explaining herself to a gardener? What had she been doing in the Sports Pavilion?

He waited until she was out of sight, then left his work and looked inside the Sports Pavilion himself. He couldn't see anything unusual. 'All the same,' he thought, 'she was doing something in there.'

As he came out again, he bumped into Ann Shapland. 'Have you seen Miss Bulstrode?' she asked.

'She was talking to Briggs just now, Miss, but I think she's gone back to the house,' replied Adam.

Ann frowned. 'What were you doing in the Sports Pavilion?' she asked.

'I was just looking,' Adam said in a rude voice. 'I'm allowed to look, aren't I?'

'I think you should get on with your work,' said Ann, and walked back towards the school. When she turned round, Adam was busy repairing the wire netting.

CHAPTER 8

MURDER

One night the telephone rang at the local police station. The Sergeant who answered quickly wrote down some details, and then hurried off to find his colleagues.

'A murder at Meadowbank school?' said Detective Inspector Kelsey, greatly surprised. 'Who's been murdered?'

'The Games teacher, sir,' said the Sergeant. 'Her name's Miss Springer. She's been found shot dead in the school's Sports Pavilion.'

'Did they find the gun?' asked Kelsey.

'No, sir.'

'Interesting,' said Detective Inspector Kelsey. He called his team together, and they left quickly to do their job.

♦ ◆ ♦

At Meadowbank Inspector Kelsey was met by Miss Bulstrode. 'What would you like to do first, Inspector,' she asked, 'visit the Sports Pavilion or hear the full details?'

'If someone could show the doctor and my two Sergeants where the body is,' replied Kelsey, 'I'd like a few words with you first.'

'Certainly.' Miss Bulstrode arranged everything without fuss. 'Come with me.'

'Who found the body?' asked Kelsey, as he followed Miss Bulstrode into her sitting room.

'Miss Johnson, the matron,' said Miss Bulstrode.

'I'll talk to her in a minute,' Kelsey said. 'First, can you tell me about the murdered woman?'

'Her name is Grace Springer – she was new this term.'

'And what do you know about her?'

'I hadn't met her before this term, but her references were excellent,' said Miss Bulstrode.

'Have you got any idea at all why this happened? Was she unhappy? Was she seeing anyone – a man, perhaps?'

Miss Bulstrode shook her head. 'Not that I know of,' she replied. 'And it seems very unlikely. She was not that kind of woman.'

'Was there any reason why Miss Springer should be in the Sports Pavilion at night?' continued Kelsey.

'No reason at all,' said Miss Bulstrode.

'Very well, Miss Bulstrode. I'll talk to Miss Johnson now.'

Miss Johnson had been given a lot of <u>brandy</u> to drink after her discovery of the body, which made her talk a lot. 'Such an awful thing to happen,' she said to Inspector Kelsey. 'I can't believe it. Miss Springer was so – well, so sure of herself. The sort of woman who could deal with a burglar all by herself.'

'A burglar?' said Inspector Kelsey. 'Was there anything to steal in the Sports Pavilion?'

'Well, no, not really – just swimsuits and sports equipment.'

'Were there any signs of a <u>break-in</u>?' asked the Inspector.

'I don't really know,' said Miss Johnson. 'The door was open when we got there and—'

'There were no signs of a break-in,' interrupted Miss Bulstrode.

'I see,' said Kelsey. 'Someone used a key.' He looked at Miss Johnson. 'Did people like Miss Springer?' he asked.

'I don't think so,' said Miss Johnson slowly. 'She was very sure of herself – sometimes quite rude – and was quite nosey.'

'Now, Miss Johnson,' said Kelsey. 'Tell me exactly what happened.'

'It was late, and I was up with one of our pupils, who was ill. I looked out of the window and saw a light in the Sports Pavilion. It was moving about.'

'So it was a torch?'

'Yes, it must have been. I didn't think of burglars. I thought it was one of our pupils – meeting a boy, perhaps. I didn't want to disturb Miss Bulstrode, so I went to ask Miss Chadwick to come with me and see what was going on. We went out by the side door and were standing on the path, when we heard a shot from the Sports Pavilion. We ran there as fast as we could. The door was open, and we switched on the light and—'

Kelsey interrupted. 'So the Sports Pavilion was dark when you got there?'

'Yes. We switched on the light and there she was. She—'

'That's all right,' said Inspector Kelsey kindly, 'I'll go and see for myself. Did you meet anyone, or hear anyone running away?'

'No, we didn't,' said Miss Johnson.

'Well, thank you,' said Inspector Kelsey. 'That's very clear. I'll go out to the Sports Pavilion now.'

'I'll come with you,' said Miss Bulstrode, and led Inspector Kelsey out to the Sports Pavilion, where the police were busy.

As the Inspector entered the Pavilion, he could see the girls' lockers, a stand for tennis racquets and hockey sticks, and a door that led off to the showers and changing rooms. The police photographer and the officer testing for fingerprints had just finished.

The police doctor was kneeling by the body, and looked up as Kelsey approached. 'She was shot from about four feet away,' said the doctor. 'The bullet went through the heart and killed her immediately.'

'How long ago?'

'About an hour ago,' replied the doctor.

Kelsey nodded, and went to talk to Miss Chadwick, who was standing against the wall. She was very calm.

'Miss Chadwick?' he said. 'You and Miss Johnson discovered the body. Do you know what time it was?'

'It was ten minutes to one when Miss Johnson woke me.'

Kelsey nodded. He looked down at the dead woman. Her bright red hair was short and she had a thin, athletic body. She was wearing a dark heavy skirt and sweater.

'Have you found the gun?' asked Kelsey.

'No, sir,' said one of his men. 'But there is a torch with the dead woman's fingerprints on it.'

'So Miss Springer had the torch,' said Kelsey thoughtfully. 'Any idea why she was here?' he asked Miss Chadwick.

'No,' replied Miss Chadwick, shaking her head. 'No idea at all. Perhaps she came to find something she'd forgotten – though it seems rather late to do that.'

Kelsey looked around him. Nothing seemed disturbed except the stand of tennis racquets, several of which were lying around on the floor.

'Perhaps,' continued Miss Chadwick, 'Miss Springer saw a light and came to investigate, like we did. She was confident enough to do that on her own.'

'Was the side door of the house unlocked?'

'Yes,' said Miss Chadwick. 'Miss Springer probably unlocked it.'

Inspector Kelsey turned back to Miss Bulstrode, who was standing by the door. 'So, Miss Springer saw a light in the Sports Pavilion and came to investigate. And then she was shot.'

'But why would someone shoot her?' said Miss Bulstrode. 'Surely they would just run away? There's nothing here worth stealing, and certainly nothing worth murdering for.'

'So do you think that Miss Springer interrupted a meeting of some kind? A local boy, perhaps?'

'That seems more likely,' said Miss Bulstrode. 'Except local boys – and the girls in my school – don't have guns...'

CHAPTER 9

CAT AMONG THE <u>PIGEONS</u>[5]

Letter from Jennifer Sutcliffe to her mother:

Dear Mummy,

We had a murder last night – Miss Springer, the Games teacher. It happened in the middle of the night and the police came and this morning they're asking everybody questions.

We were told not to talk about it but I thought you'd like to know.

With love,

Jennifer

◆ ◆ ◆

Miss Bulstrode knew some important people, so very little about Miss Springer's murder appeared in the newspapers. Ann Shapland was busy, sending letters to the girls' parents telling them what happened. And Miss Bulstrode had a meeting with Inspector Kelsey.

'We'll search the school to try to find the gun,' Inspector Kelsey told her. 'And we'll need to interview the staff and the pupils. Until we're finished, you can't use the Sports Pavilion, I'm afraid.'

'I'll ask the girls if they know anything about Miss Springer's death,' said Miss Bulstrode. 'I'll let you know if they tell me anything.'

◆ ◆ ◆

'I've looked through all the lockers in the Sports Pavilion, sir,' said the Sergeant. 'None of them were locked. But I didn't find anything important.'

Kelsey looked around thoughtfully. The hockey sticks and tennis racquets had been replaced tidily on their stands.

'Oh well,' he said, 'I'm going up to the house now to have a talk with the staff.'

'Do you think it was one of them, sir?'

'It could have been,' said Kelsey. 'Nobody's got an <u>alibi</u> except Miss Chadwick and Miss Johnson. Everyone has separate rooms, so if they say they were asleep in bed, we don't know if they're lying. Anyone could have met Miss Springer or followed her to the Sports Pavilion. After shooting her, they could easily come back to the house without being seen. But we need a motive – *why* was Miss Springer shot?'

Kelsey walked slowly back to the house. Old Briggs, the gardener, stopped working as the Inspector approached.

'You're working late,' Kelsey said to him, smiling. 'But I can see you do a good job – the gardens here are very well looked after.'

'It's hard work,' said Briggs, 'but it's easier now I've got a strong young man to help me.'

'Have you got a new gardener?' Kelsey asked.

'Yes, I have,' said Briggs. 'Adam Goodman, his name is. Came and asked for a job. He's been here since the start of term.'

'He's not on my list of people who work here,' replied Kelsey sharply.

'You can talk to him tomorrow,' said Briggs. 'But I'm sure he can't tell you anything.'

That evening Miss Bulstrode spoke to the girls about Miss Springer's death. 'Please come and tell me,' she said, 'if Miss Springer said anything to you that could be important.'

'I wish we did know something,' said Julia Upjohn sadly, as she and Jennifer Sutcliffe went back to their rooms. 'But Miss Springer always seemed so ordinary.'

◆ ◆ ◆

Inspector Kelsey was interviewing the teachers. He started with Miss Vansittart, but she hadn't seen or noticed anything. Miss Springer had been good at her job, but she was rude and people didn't like her very much.

The next teacher was Eileen Rich, who said that she hadn't heard or noticed Miss Springer say anything important. But when Kelsey asked if there was anyone who didn't like – or even hated – Miss Springer, he got an answer he didn't expect.

'Oh no,' said Eileen Rich. 'She just wasn't important enough to hate. She annoyed people but nothing she did really mattered. I think she knew that, and that's why she was so rude, and eager to find out people's secrets. She tried to make herself important, but she just *wasn't*. I'm sure she wasn't killed for herself – she was probably in the wrong place at the wrong time.'

'I see,' said Inspector Kelsey. 'Did you like her, Miss Rich?'

'I never really thought about her. I know it's a horrible thing to say, but she was just the Games teacher.'

Kelsey looked at her curiously. She was a strange young woman, he thought.

'How long have you been at Meadowbank?' he asked.

'Just over a year and a half.'

'Has there ever been any trouble here before?'

'Oh no. Everything's been all right until this term.'

'What else has been wrong this term?' Kelsey asked quickly.

'I don't know if I can explain,' Eileen Rich said slowly. 'But I do feel that there's someone here who's wrong – someone who doesn't belong.' She looked at him. 'There's a cat among the pigeons. We're the pigeons, all of us, and the cat's among us. But we don't know who the cat is...'

Chapter 10

Fantastic story

Inspector Kelsey next talked to Mademoiselle Angèle Blanche. She was about thirty-five with neat brown hair, and she wore a plain coat and skirt. It was her first term at Meadowbank, she explained. She had been a teacher in France, but this was her first time in England. She didn't think she would stay at Meadowbank for another term. 'It is not nice to be in a school where murders take place,' she said.

'Did you know Miss Springer well?' Inspector Kelsey asked.

'No,' said Mademoiselle Blanche. 'She had bad manners and a loud voice – and she was rude to me. She did not like it when I went to the Sports Pavilion. I was looking around and she told me that I should not be there. She spoke to me as if I was a pupil, not a teacher.'

'That must have been annoying,' said Kelsey.

'And then she shouts at me,' continued Mademoiselle Blanche. 'I had picked up the key to the door and forgot to put it back. Did she think I was going to steal it? She had the manners of a pig! The other teachers, at least they are polite.'

After answering a few more questions, Mademoiselle Blanche left the room.

'So, Miss Springer didn't like people visiting the Sports Pavilion,' said Kelsey. 'I wonder why? Was she hiding something there? Oh well, let's see the rest of the staff.'

Miss Blake was young and serious with a round, good-natured face. She had nothing to say that could help. She had seen very little of Miss Springer and had no idea of what could have led to her death.

All Miss Rowan said was that Miss Springer was very rude, and had hinted that in other schools she had discovered people's secrets.

Next Inspector Kelsey saw Ann Shapland. He approved of her neat and business-like appearance.

'Well, Miss Shapland,' he said. 'Can you tell me anything about Miss Springer's death?'

'I'm afraid not,' said Ann. 'I have my own sitting room, and I don't see much of the other staff. And even now I still can't believe what happened. Why would anyone want to break into the Sports Pavilion and shoot Miss Springer? Why didn't they just run away?'

Thinking of what Mademoiselle Blanche had said, Kelsey asked, 'I've been told that Miss Springer didn't like people visiting the Sports Pavilion. Did she say anything to you?'

'No,' said Ann Shapland, 'but I've only been to the Pavilion once or twice. Though I did hear that Miss Springer was quite rude to Mademoiselle Blanche about it.'

'Do you know anything about Miss Springer's private life?'

'No,' replied Ann. 'I don't think anyone did.'

'And is there anything else – perhaps about the Sports Pavilion – that you can tell me?'

'Well…' Ann hesitated. 'I did see the new gardener coming out of there once. He shouldn't have been in there – he was supposed to be working.' She frowned. 'And he was rude to me.'

Kelsey made a note of this after Ann left. Then he questioned the school servants, but learned nothing helpful, before he was interrupted by Miss Bulstrode.

'Princess Shaista – one of our foreign pupils – would like to speak to you, Inspector,' she said. 'She's the niece of the <u>Emir</u> Ibrahim, and thinks she's quite an important person.'

A slim, dark girl of medium height came in. 'You are the police?' she asked.

'Yes, that's right,' said Kelsey, smiling. 'Please tell me what you know about Miss Springer.'

'I will tell you,' said Shaista. 'There are people here watching this place.' She lowered her voice dramatically. 'They want to kidnap me. Then they will ask my uncle for a lot of money – a <u>ransom</u> – before they let me go.'

This was not what Kelsey had expected. 'Er – well – perhaps,' he said doubtfully. 'But – even if this is true – what has it got to do with the death of Miss Springer?'

'She must have found out about them,' said Shaista. She sounded as if she was enjoying herself. 'Perhaps she asked them for money to keep silent. They meet at the Sports Pavilion, but instead of giving her money they shoot her.'

'Well – er…' said Inspector Kelsey, 'I don't know what to say.' He paused. 'Is this your own idea,' he asked, 'or did Miss Springer say something about it?'

'The only thing Miss Springer ever said to me was "Run faster",' said Shaista sulkily.

'So it's possible that you're imagining all this?' Kelsey suggested gently.

Shaista was very annoyed. 'You do not understand! My cousin was Prince Ali Yusuf of Ramat. He was killed in the revolution. I was going to marry him when I was older, so I am an important person. Perhaps these people think I know where the jewels are.'

'What jewels?' said Kelsey with surprise.

'My cousin, Prince Ali, had many jewels, worth much money,' Shaista said calmly. 'They disappeared in the revolution. I was Ali's nearest relation, and now he is dead the jewels belong to me.'

Inspector Kelsey wasn't sure what to believe. 'Has anyone said anything to you about these jewels?' he asked.

'No,' admitted Shaista.

Inspector Kelsey made a decision. 'I think,' he said pleasantly, 'that you're talking nonsense.'

Shaista looked at him angrily. 'I am just telling you what I know,' she said, standing up and walking out of the door.

'Kidnapping and wonderful jewels!' said Kelsey to himself. 'What next?'

CHAPTER 11

CONFERENCE

When Inspector Kelsey returned to the police station, Adam Goodman was waiting for him. The young gardener looked sulky and rude, but when he was alone with Inspector Kelsey his behaviour changed. He was quiet and polite as he showed the Inspector his identification.

'So *that's* who you are,' said Kelsey. 'What are you doing working at a girls' school?' Adam explained that he was here to watch Princess Shaista and see if anyone contacted her.

Kelsey listened with interest. 'So the girl was telling the truth?' he said with surprise. 'I didn't believe her. But you say that there *are* jewels – jewels worth a million pounds! You must admit it's hard to believe.' He paused. 'So who do these jewels belong to?'

'The lawyers would argue about that for years,' said Adam. 'They may belong to Prince Ali Yusuf's family, or he may have left them to someone else. The truth is, whoever finds the jewels will just keep them – and there are a lot of people looking for them.'

'But why is Meadowbank involved? Because of Princess Shaista?'

'That's right,' said Adam. 'Princess Shaista is Ali Yusuf's cousin. Someone may try to contact her or give her the jewels. We know there's a well-known secret agent staying in a local hotel. She just finds out useful information – nothing against the law. But we've been told that there's another woman in the area – a woman who was a dancer in Ramat when the revolution started. She works for a foreign government, but we don't know where she is or even what she looks like.'

49

Kelsey shook his head. 'This all sounds unbelievable,' he said. 'Secret agents, jewels, murder – they don't happen in real life!'

'I know what you mean,' said Adam. 'It doesn't seem possible – but it *is* happening. And it's happening here.'

There was a silence, and then Inspector Kelsey asked, 'What do you think happened last night?'

'I don't know,' Adam said slowly. 'Why was Miss Springer in the Sports Pavilion at night? Did she go there to meet someone? Did she follow someone there? Or did she see a light and go and investigate?'

'Everyone says that Miss Springer was very sure of herself,' said Kelsey. 'And that she was nosey. I think that she either went to investigate – or to meet someone from the school. Miss Rich, one of the teachers, says that there's someone here who doesn't belong – a cat among the pigeons.'

'A cat among the pigeons,' repeated Adam. 'That's a good description.'

'If there *is* a cat among the pigeons,' said Kelsey, 'it's more likely to be one of the three new staff. Miss Springer is dead, so that leaves either Miss Shapland or Mademoiselle Blanche.' He looked towards Adam. 'Any ideas?'

'I saw Mademoiselle Blanche coming out of the Sports Pavilion one day,' said Adam. 'She looked guilty. But I think it's more likely to be Miss Shapland. She's cool and intelligent.'

Kelsey smiled. 'Ann Shapland was suspicious of *you*,' he said. 'She saw you coming out of the Sports Pavilion and said you were rude to her.' He paused. 'We need to find out what's happening at Meadowbank,' he said. 'I think I'll tell Miss Bulstrode who you are. She's an impressive woman – and she won't tell anyone.'

Adam nodded. 'Yes,' he said. 'Tell her who I am.'

CHAPTER 12

NEW LAMPS FOR OLD

Miss Bulstrode listened carefully to Inspector Kelsey and Adam as they explained the whole story. 'Very interesting,' she said calmly, when they had finished. 'And will you still be my gardener?' she asked Adam.

'If you don't mind,' he replied. 'Then I can keep an eye on things.'

'I hope you're not expecting another murder,' said Miss Bulstrode. 'I don't think Meadowbank could survive two murders in one term.'

'No, no,' said Inspector Kelsey. 'And we don't want any news about this in the papers. We'll say that Miss Springer went to catch some burglars, who then shot her by accident.'

'And have you finished with the Sports Pavilion?' Miss Bulstrode asked. 'We'd like to use it again if we can.'

'You'll be able to use it again soon. We've searched the place – and found nothing.' He paused. 'There's only one more thing I have to ask you. Has anything happened this term that's made you worried or uneasy?'

Miss Bulstrode was silent for a moment. 'I have had a feeling that something is wrong,' she said slowly. 'But I don't know exactly what it is.' She paused. 'I think that I missed something important on the first day of term.' She explained about Mrs Upjohn and the <u>drunken</u> Lady Veronica Carlton.

Adam was interested. 'So Mrs Upjohn looked out of the front window and recognized someone,' he said. 'Then later she was talking about her work during the war, and secret agents.'

'Yes, that's right,' said Miss Bulstrode.

'We need to talk to Mrs Upjohn,' said Kelsey. 'As soon as possible.'

'I think she's travelling abroad at the moment,' said Miss Bulstrode. 'Let me ask her daughter, Julia.' She pressed the buzzer on her desk. When there was no answer, she stepped out of her room for a moment and asked a passing girl to get Julia Upjohn.

'I should go before she gets here,' Adam said. 'I'm only the gardener.' He stood up. 'And Miss Bulstrode,' he added, 'will it be all right if I become very friendly with some of your staff – Mademoiselle Blanche, for example?'

Miss Bulstrode looked unhappy, but agreed. 'I suppose you must do everything you can.'

'And if I meet some of the girls in the garden, I'm only trying to get information,' Adam said, before he left. 'They may know something.'

Soon Julia Upjohn knocked at the door. 'Come in, Julia,' said Miss Bulstrode. 'I just wanted to ask for your mother's address – I need to contact her.'

'But mother's gone to Anatolia – in Turkey,' Julia explained. 'On a bus.'

'On a bus?' said Miss Bulstrode with surprise.

Julia nodded. 'Mother likes travelling like that,' she said. 'It's uncomfortable, but cheap. She'll probably arrive in the city of Van in about three weeks.'

'I see,' said Miss Bulstrode. 'Tell me, Julia, did your mother ever say that she'd seen someone here – at Meadowbank – who she knew during the war?'

'No, Miss Bulstrode. I'm sure she didn't.'

'Well, thank you, Julia. That's all.'

◆ ◆ ◆

Jennifer Sutcliffe walked away from the tennis courts, swinging her racquet. She was annoyed that she had played badly – she was very serious about tennis.

'Excuse me—'

Jennifer looked up, surprised to see a well-dressed blonde woman, wearing a blue dress and a big hat, standing on the path. The woman was holding a long, flat package. It was as if she had just stepped out from behind the hedge – but Jennifer didn't think of that.

The woman spoke with an American accent. 'I wonder if you can tell me where I can find a girl called – she looked at a piece of paper – 'Jennifer Sutcliffe?'

'*I'm* Jennifer Sutcliffe,' said Jennifer with surprise.

'Well, isn't that extraordinary?' the woman said. 'You're just the girl I want to see. Let me explain. I was at lunch yesterday with your aunt – or was it your <u>godmother</u>? – I'm afraid I can't remember her name. But anyway, she knew I was coming to Meadowbank and asked me to give you this new tennis racquet. She said you'd been asking for one.'

Jennifer was delighted. 'It must have been my aunt – Aunt Gina, Mrs Campbell.'

'Yes, I remember now. That was the name. Campbell.' The woman gave Jennifer the package.

Jennifer opened it quickly. 'Oh, it's wonderful!' she exclaimed, as she saw the brand new tennis racquet. 'Thank you so much for bringing it!'

'It was no trouble,' the woman said. 'And your aunt asked me to bring your old racquet back with me – for restringing.' She picked up the racquet that Jennifer had dropped.

'I don't think it's really worth restringing,' said Jennifer, but without paying much attention. She was swinging her new racquet and wanted to try it.

'But an extra racquet is always useful,' said the woman. 'Oh dear,' she said, looking at her watch. 'It's much later than I thought. I must go now. It was nice to meet you.'

She ran along the path towards the gate.

'Thank you very much,' Jennifer called out after her, before going inside to find Julia.

'Look at my new tennis racquet!' she said to her friend. 'Aunt Gina sent it to me.' She showed it to Julia. 'Isn't it lovely?'

Julia admired the new racquet. 'What have you done with the old one?'

'Oh, the woman took it. She met Aunt Gina at lunch. Aunt Gina wanted the old racquet so she can restring it.'

Julia frowned. 'But your racquet didn't need restringing.'

'Oh, it did, Julia. The strings were very loose.'

'But it was *my* racquet that needed restringing,' said Julia. 'You said your racquet – the one I have now – had already been restrung.'

'Yes, that's true,' said Jennifer in surprise. 'Perhaps Aunt Gina just thought that if I wanted a new racquet, it was because the old one needed restringing. What does it matter?'

'I suppose it doesn't really matter,' said Julia slowly. 'But I do think it's strange. It's like the story of <u>Aladdin</u> – you know – like new lamps for old[6].'

CHAPTER 13

CATASTROPHE

It was the third weekend of term. There were only about twenty girls left behind at Meadowbank, because this weekend parents were allowed to come and take their daughters out for the day. Some of the staff were also away for the weekend. Miss Bulstrode herself had decided to go and stay with the <u>Duchess</u> of Welsham at her house in the country².

On Saturday morning, before she left, Miss Bulstrode was dictating some final letters to Ann Shapland. When the phone rang, Ann answered. 'It's the Emir Ibrahim's secretary,' she told Miss Bulstrode. 'The Emir's arrived in London and would like to take Shaista out tomorrow.'

Miss Bulstrode took the phone and spoke to the Emir's secretary. Shaista would be ready at eleven-thirty on Sunday morning, she said. The girl must be back at the school by 8 pm.

She put down the phone. 'And that's the last letter,' she said to Ann. 'Type them up and send them, and then you're free for the weekend.'

'Thank you, Miss Bulstrode,' Ann said.

'Enjoy yourself, my dear.'

'I will,' said Ann.

'Are you meeting a young man?'

'Well – yes.' Ann's face turned a little red. 'But it's not serious – only an old friend.'

Miss Chadwick hurried in, and Ann went back to her office.

'The Emir Ibrahim, Shaista's uncle, is taking her out tomorrow,' Miss Bulstrode told her friend. 'He probably won't come himself, but if he does, tell him Shaista is doing well.'

'She's not very clever,' said Miss Chadwick.

'Not in some ways,' said Miss Bulstrode. 'But in other ways she's very grown up. Sometimes she sounds like a woman of twenty-five – she's led such a varied life and visited so many different countries. Perhaps in this country we keep our children young for too long.'

'I'll go and tell Shaista about her uncle,' said Miss Chadwick. 'Go and enjoy your weekend, and don't worry about anything.'

'Oh, I won't worry,' said Miss Bulstrode. 'Eleanor Vansittart is in charge – and with you here too, Chaddy, nothing will go wrong.'

◆ ◆ ◆

By ten o'clock on Sunday morning only Miss Vansittart, Miss Chadwick, Miss Rowan and Mademoiselle Blanche were left at Meadowbank. Miss Bulstrode and Ann Shapland had left on Saturday, and Miss Johnson, Miss Rich and Miss Blake had left earlier that morning.

At about half-past eleven cars began to arrive at the school as parents came to take their daughters out for the day. Miss Vansittart greeted the mothers with a smile, and answered their questions about the recent tragedy.

'It was terrible, quite terrible,' she said. 'But we don't talk about it too much. We don't want the girls to worry.'

Julia Upjohn and Jennifer Sutcliffe were looking out the window. 'I wish someone was coming to take me out,' said Julia, as they watched people come and go.

'Mummy couldn't come today,' said Jennifer. 'Daddy's got some important visitors. But she's taking me out next weekend. You can come too, if you like. I told Mummy I'd like to bring a friend.'

'I'd love to,' said Julia. She looked out the window again. 'Look at Shaista,' she said. 'She's all dressed up for London. And look how high the heels of her shoes are!' A driver wearing a smart uniform was opening the door of a large luxury car. Shaista got in and the car drove away.

'So what shall we do this afternoon?' asked Jennifer. 'I don't need to write a letter to Mummy, because I'll see her next week. And I can't really think of anything to say. She got quite upset when I told her about the murder.'

'I can always think of lots to say,' said Julia, 'but I don't have anyone to write to.'

'What about your mother?'

'I told you – she's gone to Anatolia on a bus. She's left me a list of places to write to, but she won't get my letters for a while.' She paused. 'I wonder why Miss Bulstrode wanted to contact her. Perhaps it's about Miss Springer. I think there are a lot of things they haven't told us about Miss Springer,' Julia added thoughtfully. 'There are definitely strange things happening here – like your new tennis racquet.'

'Oh, I meant to tell you,' said Jennifer, 'I wrote and thanked Aunt Gina and this morning I got a letter from her saying she was glad I'd got a new racquet but that she never sent it to me.'

'I told you it was strange,' said Julia. 'And your house was burgled too, wasn't it?'

'Yes, but they didn't take anything.'

'That just makes it even more interesting,' said Julia. 'I think,' she added thoughtfully, 'that we'll probably have a second murder soon.'

'Oh Julia – why should we have a second murder?' said Jennifer.

'Well, there's usually a second murder in books,' said Julia. 'You must be careful, Jennifer, that you're not murdered next.'

'Me?' said Jennifer, surprised. 'Why should anyone murder me?'

'Because you seem to be involved in whatever's happening,' Julia said. 'We must ask your mother some questions next week. Perhaps she was given something in Ramat…'

◆ ◆ ◆

'Where's Shaista?' Miss Rowan asked Miss Vansittart and Miss Chadwick. 'I can't find her anywhere. The Emir's car has just arrived to take her to London.'

'What?' Miss Chadwick looked up, surprised. 'But the Emir's car collected Shaista at eleven-thirty. I saw her leave myself.'

Eleanor Vansittart went out to speak to the driver. 'There must be a mistake,' she said. 'The young lady has already left for London. Perhaps the car was ordered twice?'

The driver didn't seem very surprised. 'It does happen,' he admitted. 'Sometimes two different people ring up and both book a car by mistake.'

Miss Vansittart looked a little doubtful as she watched him drive away, but she decided there was nothing to worry about.

The afternoon was peaceful, and the girls who were left went swimming and played tennis. Miss Vansittart sat outside under a tree and wrote some letters.

At half-past four the telephone rang, and Miss Chadwick answered. 'This is the Emir's secretary speaking from London,' a man's voice said.

'Oh yes,' said Miss Chadwick. 'Is it about Shaista?'

'Yes,' said the secretary. 'The Emir is annoyed he was not told that Shaista was not coming today.'

'Wasn't coming!' said Miss Chadwick. 'What do you mean? Hasn't Shaista arrived?'

'No, she hasn't.'

'But a car collected her this morning at eleven-thirty.'

'That's very strange,' said the secretary. 'I'll ring up the car company at once and see what's happened.'

'Oh dear,' said Miss Chadwick, 'I do hope there hasn't been an accident.'

'Oh, don't worry,' said the secretary cheerfully. 'We'd know by now. I suppose—' he hesitated.

'Yes?' said Miss Chadwick.

'Well, I was going to ask if Shaista had gone to meet a boyfriend.'

'Certainly not,' said Miss Chadwick. 'It's quite impossible.'

But as she put the phone down, she wondered. Was it impossible? You never really knew what girls would do.

She went to find Miss Vansittart and told her what had happened. 'Do you think we should call the police?' Miss Chadwick asked. 'Shaista did say that someone might try to kidnap her.'

'Kidnap her? Nonsense!' said Miss Vansittart sharply. 'Miss Bulstrode left me in charge and I certainly won't call the police.'

Miss Chadwick looked at her slowly. She thought Miss Vansittart was being very stupid. She went to the phone and tried to call Miss Bulstrode at the Duchess of Welsham's country house. Unfortunately everyone was out.

Chapter 14

Miss Chadwick lies awake

Shaista had not returned by eight o'clock, and there was no news of her. Miss Chadwick had rung Inspector Kelsey, who said he would deal with it. He didn't sound worried.

But Miss Chadwick was worried. That night she lay in bed, unable to sleep. She kept thinking about kidnapping – and murder. It was terrible that such things could happen at her <u>beloved</u> Meadowbank. She loved the school so much. She didn't want Miss Bulstrode to retire when everything was going so well. Though after the murder, perhaps parents would take their children away...

With a sigh, Miss Chadwick sat up, switched on the light and looked at her watch. It was just after a quarter to one. Just about the time that poor Miss Springer... No, she wouldn't think about that.

She got out of bed and went to get a drink of water. On her way back to bed she lifted the curtain and looked out of the window.

There was a light in the Sports Pavilion.

Miss Chadwick quickly got dressed and picked up a torch. She rushed down the stairs and out towards the Sports Pavilion. She didn't stop to wake anyone else – all she wanted to do was find out who was there. She did, however, stop to pick up a weapon. She walked quietly to the open door of the Sports Pavilion, pushed it fully open and looked in...

◆ ◆ ◆

At the same time as Miss Chadwick got out of bed, Ann Shapland, looking very attractive in a black evening dress, was sitting at a table in a fashionable London restaurant. She smiled at the young man sitting opposite her. Dear Dennis, she thought, he's always the same.

'How's your new job?' Dennis asked.

'I'm rather enjoying it, actually,' said Ann.

'I didn't think you'd like working in a school,' Dennis said.

'I'd hate to be a teacher,' Ann said, 'but I like being a secretary at Meadowbank. Miss Bulstrode is a very impressive woman. I don't dare make any mistakes!'

'I wish you'd stop working, Ann, and marry me instead.'

'I'm not ready to do that yet,' Ann replied. 'And of course I have to think about my mother. Sometimes, when she gets really bad, I have to leave my job and go and look after her.'

'I think it's wonderful,' said Dennis, 'that you take such good care of your mother. Of course I've never met her, but wouldn't she be better living in an old people's home?'

'No,' said Ann <u>firmly</u>. 'Mother's happy most of the time. But sometimes she forgets who she is and where she is. She has a nice woman who looks after her, and when Mother gets too difficult, I go and help.'

'But don't you mind giving up your jobs?'

'No, not really,' replied Ann. 'I like doing different things. And I don't like to stay in one job for too long.'

'I'm sure you won't stay too long at Meadowbank,' said Dennis. 'You'll get tired of all those women.'

'There's a very good-looking gardener,' said Ann. She laughed when she saw Dennis's expression. 'Don't worry. I'm only trying to make you jealous.'

'Tell me about the murder,' Dennis said. 'It was the Games teacher, wasn't it?'

'Yes.' Ann became serious. 'It was all very strange,' she said thoughtfully. 'I've been thinking about it, and I do know one piece of information that's rather interesting.'

'Ann!'

'Oh, don't worry,' Ann said. 'It doesn't seem to fit in with anything properly. Perhaps there'll be a second murder,' she added cheerfully. 'That might help me understand better.'

At exactly that moment, back at Meadowbank, Miss Chadwick pushed open the door of the Sports Pavilion.

CHAPTER 15

MURDER REPEATS ITSELF

'Come along,' said Inspector Kelsey, entering the room with a grim face. 'There's been another murder.' He and Adam Goodman had been having a drink and talking about the case when the telephone rang.

'Who is it?' asked Adam, as he followed Inspector Kelsey down the stairs.

'Another teacher, Miss Vansittart – in the Sports Pavilion.'

'The Sports Pavilion again?' said Adam. 'Why is that place so important?'

◆ ◆ ◆

It was like a bad dream repeating itself, thought Kelsey, as he entered the Sports Pavilion and saw the doctor kneeling next to a dead body.

'She was killed about half an hour ago,' the doctor told him.

'Who found her?' said Kelsey.

'Miss Chadwick, sir,' said his Sergeant. 'She saw a light, came out to investigate and found her dead. She's very upset. It was the matron, Miss Johnson, who rang us.'

'And how was Miss Vansittart killed?' Kelsey asked the doctor. 'Was she shot, too?'

The doctor shook his head. 'No. She was hit on the back of the head. She was probably kneeling down and someone hit her with something heavy. No – that wasn't the weapon,' he added, as Inspector Kelsey looked at a golf club lying near the door. 'She was hit with something like a <u>sandbag</u>.'

'So, she was kneeling in front of this locker,' said Kelsey. He looked at it closely. 'This is Princess Shaista's locker – the girl who's missing. Do we know anything about her yet?'

'No, sir,' said his Sergeant. 'The car hasn't been found. But the police in London have been told.'

'Why has this girl been kidnapped?' asked the doctor.

'I don't know,' said Kelsey <u>gloomily</u>. 'When she told me she was afraid of being kidnapped I didn't believe her.' He looked around. 'Well,' he said, 'carry on with the photographs and the fingerprints. I'm going to the house.'

He was met by Miss Johnson, the matron, who was upset but in control of herself. 'This is terrible, Inspector,' she said. 'Two of our teachers killed! Poor Miss Chadwick is very upset. The doctor gave her something to calm her down.'

'Before I talk to her, can you tell me the last time you saw Miss Vansittart?'

'I haven't seen her at all today,' said Miss Johnson. 'I've been away all day. I arrived back at eleven and went straight up to my room.'

'Did you look out of your window towards the Sports Pavilion?' Kelsey asked.

'No, I'm afraid not,' said Miss Johnson. 'I had a bath and went to bed. I was asleep when Miss Chadwick came in. She looked as white as a ghost and was shaking all over.'

'Was Miss Vansittart here all day today?'

'Yes, I think so. Miss Bulstrode is away, and left her in charge.'

'And who else was here?'

Miss Johnson thought for a moment. 'Miss Vansittart, Miss Chadwick, Mademoiselle Blanche and Miss Rowan.'

'I see,' said Inspector Kelsey. 'Well, I'd like to talk to Miss Chadwick now.'

Miss Chadwick was sitting in a chair, with her legs covered up to keep her warm. She looked shocked, white and ill. 'Is she really dead? Is there any chance that – that she might recover?'

Kelsey shook his head slowly.

'It's so awful,' said Miss Chadwick. She burst into tears. 'This will ruin the school,' she said. 'This will ruin Meadowbank. I can't bear it – I can't bear it.'

'I know this has been a terrible shock for you, Miss Chadwick,' said Kelsey, 'but I want you to be brave and tell me what happened.'

'I – I went to bed early, but I couldn't sleep. I was worried about Shaista – she's still missing. Eventually – it was about quarter to one – I got up for a glass of water and looked out of the window. And I saw a light moving, like a torch, in the Sports Pavilion.'

'Yes. And then?'

'And then,' said Miss Chadwick, 'I was determined to see who was there and what they were doing. So I got dressed and hurried out before they could get away. The door wasn't shut and I pushed it open. And there she was – dead.'

She began to shake all over.

'Yes, yes, Miss Chadwick, it's all right,' said Kelsey. 'Just one more question. Did you take a golf club with you? Or did Miss Vansittart take it?'

'A golf club?' said Miss Chadwick uncertainly. 'I can't remember – oh, yes, I think I picked it up in the hall. I took it out with me as a weapon. I must have dropped it when I saw Eleanor. I somehow got back to the house and woke Miss Johnson. Oh! I can't bear it. I can't bear it – this will be the end of Meadowbank…'

Inspector Kelsey left Miss Chadwick to the care of Miss Johnson. As he went downstairs, he noticed a pile of sandbags by the side door, and thought that one of them could easily have

Agatha Christie

been used to kill Miss Vansittart. Perhaps someone in the house
had picked up the sandbag, murdered Miss Vansittart – and put it
back afterwards...

CHAPTER 16

THE RIDDLE OF THE SPORTS PAVILION

Miss Bulstrode sat calmly at her desk as the telephone rang over and over again. Each time it was a parent ringing to say they were taking their daughter away from Meadowbank.

Finally Miss Bulstrode made her decision. She told Ann Shapland that Meadowbank was closing until the end of term. Any girls were welcome to stay if it wasn't possible for them to go home.

'Start ringing up all the parents,' she said to Ann, 'and send them a letter.'

'Yes, Miss Bulstrode.' Ann Shapland paused before she went out. 'Excuse me,' she said. 'I know it's none of my business, but are you sure you're doing the right thing?'

'I am,' said Miss Bulstrode firmly. 'If I *tell* parents to take their children away, many of them will want the girls to stay. It's human nature. I just hope they send them back next term – if there *is* a next term.'

She looked up as Inspector Kelsey came in. 'That's your job,' she said to him. 'If you catch the murderer, then the school will survive.'

Inspector Kelsey looked unhappy. 'We're doing our best,' he said. Ann Shapland went out to start typing.

'Do you have any idea who killed my two teachers?' asked Miss Bulstrode. 'And Shaista is still missing – is there any news?'

'Not about the murders,' said Kelsey, 'but I do have news about Shaista. The Emir received a ransom note this morning. To get Shaista back safely he must leave twenty thousand pounds at the side of a local road by two o'clock tomorrow morning.' He shook his head. 'It doesn't sound very professional.' He stood up.

'What about my teachers?' asked Miss Bulstrode. 'Is there anyone I can trust?'

'We have checked them all,' said the Inspector, 'especially the new staff – Mademoiselle Blanche, Miss Springer and your secretary, Miss Shapland. Miss Shapland's previous employers have confirmed that she definitely worked for them, and she has an alibi for last night. When Miss Vansittart was killed, Miss Shapland was having dinner at a London restaurant with a man called Dennis Rathbone. The staff at the restaurant know them both. We've also checked Mademoiselle Blanche. She's worked in schools in France, and is said to be a very good teacher.

'She *could* have done both murders,' continued Kelsey, 'but we have no evidence that she did. She says she was in bed.' He paused. 'The problem is it's hard to believe that the killer is one of your staff. Miss Johnson was with her sister last night and has worked here seven years. Miss Chadwick helped you start the school. Both of them, anyway, are clear of Miss Springer's death. Miss Rich has been here over a year and last night was staying at a hotel twenty miles away. Miss Blake was with friends, and Miss Rowan has been with you for a year and has a good background.'

Miss Bulstrode nodded.

'I quite agree with you,' she said. 'So...' She paused and looked at Adam. 'It must be *you*.'

Adam's mouth opened in astonishment.

'You have a good reason for being here,' said Miss Bulstrode thoughtfully, 'and you could be working for someone else.'

'Miss Bulstrode,' said Adam with admiration, 'you think of everything!'

◆ ◆ ◆

'My goodness!' exclaimed Mrs Sutcliffe at the breakfast table. 'Henry!' She was looking at the newspaper.

'What's the matter, Joan?'

'There's been another murder! At Meadowbank! At Jennifer's school.'

'What? Let me see!' Mr Sutcliffe took the paper from his wife's hands.

'Miss Eleanor Vansittart... Sports Pavilion... same place where Miss Springer, the Games teacher... hmm...'

'I can't believe it!' said Mrs Sutcliffe. 'Meadowbank is such a good school.'

'You must go there immediately and take Jennifer away,' said her husband firmly.

'Do you think that's the right thing to do?'

'Yes, I do,' said Mr Sutcliffe. 'Go and take Jennifer away from that school – you won't be the only one.'

◆ ◆ ◆

Adam was alone in the Sports Pavilion, looking carefully in all the lockers in case the police had missed something. Suddenly he heard <u>footsteps</u>, and he quickly stepped away from the lockers and lit a cigarette.

Julia Upjohn appeared at the door. She hesitated. 'I just wanted to get my tennis racquet,' she said.

'I'm sure that's all right, Miss,' said Adam. 'The police Sergeant left me here to keep an eye on things,' he lied, 'while he went back to the police station.'

'In case the murderer comes back?' asked Julia. 'I heard that murderers always return to the scene of the crime.'

'I don't know,' said Adam. He looked at the rows of tennis racquets. 'Which one's yours?'

'It's at the end,' said Julia. 'We have our names on them,' she explained, pointing to the name labels. Adam handed Julia her racquet.

'Can I have Jennifer Sutcliffe's racquet, too?' asked Julia.

'This looks new,' said Adam, as he handed it to her.

'Yes,' said Julia. 'Her aunt sent it to her the other day. Jennifer's very good at tennis.'

She looked round. 'Do you think he will come back? The murderer?'

'I don't think so,' said Adam. 'It would be a big risk.'

'Perhaps he left something behind – a clue,' said Julia. 'That would be interesting.'

She walked out holding the two racquets.

◆ ◆ ◆

'Julia, look!' said Jennifer, as they were playing tennis. 'There's Mummy.'

The two girls turned to stare at Mrs Sutcliffe, who was walking quickly towards them, guided by Miss Rich.

'More fuss, I suppose,' said Jennifer gloomily.

'You must pack your things at once, Jennifer,' said her mother. 'I'm taking you home.'

'But – do you mean for ever?'

'Yes, I do.'

'But you can't,' said Jennifer. 'My tennis is really improving. And I like it here.'

'Don't argue with me, Jennifer,' said Mrs Sutcliffe. 'Just do as you're told.'

'But, Mummy—' Mother and daughter went towards the house, still arguing.

Suddenly Jennifer ran back to the tennis court. 'Goodbye, Julia. Mummy seems to be quite upset about these murders. I'm afraid I have to go. I'll write to you.'

'I'll write to you, too, and tell you what happens.'

'I hope they don't kill Chaddy next. I'd prefer it to be Mademoiselle Blanche, wouldn't you?'

'Yes. I wouldn't miss her very much,' said Julia. 'Did you see how angry Miss Rich looked?'

'She hasn't said anything,' said Jennifer, 'but she's angry with Mummy for taking me away.'

'Miss Rich is strange, isn't she? I've never met anyone like her before.'

'She reminds me of someone,' said Jennifer.

'I don't think she's like anybody else. She always seems to be quite unique.'

'Oh yes. She is unique. I mean to look at. But the person I saw was quite fat.'

'Jennifer!' called Mrs Sutcliffe.

'Parents can be very annoying,' said Jennifer. 'Fuss, fuss, fuss.' She said goodbye to Julia and left with her mother.

Julia walked slowly towards the Sports Pavilion, lost in thought, as the school bell rang for lunch. Suddenly she stopped and frowned, staring down at the tennis racquet she was holding, and then walked back to the house. Running upstairs to her small bedroom, she looked around, quickly lifted up the <u>mattress</u> on her bed and put the racquet underneath it. Then she went downstairs for lunch.

Chapter 17

Aladdin's Cave

It was quiet at Meadowbank that night. Lots of girls had been taken home, but those who were left were quieter and more thoughtful than usual as they went upstairs to bed.

Julia went into her bedroom and closed the door. She listened as the voices, footsteps and laughter gradually stopped and all was silent.

There was no lock on her door, so Julia put a chair underneath the door handle so she would hear if anyone tried to come in. But the girls weren't allowed in each other's rooms, and Miss Johnson, the matron, only came in if someone was ill.

Julia lifted her mattress and took out the tennis racquet. She decided to examine it now, while the lights were still on, rather than later, when a light under her door would be noticed.

There must be something hidden in the handle, thought Julia. Jennifer's house was burgled, and then there was the silly story about the new racquet – only Jennifer would believe *that*.

But Jennifer and Julia had never told anyone that they had swapped racquets, so this was the racquet that everyone was looking for in the Sports Pavilion. She looked at it carefully. There was nothing unusual about it. She used a small knife to remove the leather covering from the handle, and took off the end. There was some plasticine there, which she took out carefully – and several other things came out with it…

Julia <u>gasped</u> and stared at the beautiful, coloured red, green and blue jewels – and the shining white diamonds. She looked in wonder as she picked up the stones and let them fall through her fingers…

And then, suddenly, she heard a slight noise outside her door.

Julia sat there thinking, trying to decide what to do. She quickly picked up the jewels and put them in her wash bag, covering them with her <u>sponge</u> and soap. Then she repaired the tennis racquet, so that it looked just the same as it did before. She threw it casually down on her chair and sat on her bed, listening.

Suddenly, Julia was afraid. Two people had been killed. If anyone knew what she had found, she would be killed, too.

She managed to move a heavy desk in front of the door, and then she locked the window. At half past ten Julia turned off her light, just as usual. If anyone tries to come in, she thought, I'll knock on the wall and scream as loud as I can.

She sat on her bed, fully dressed, for a long time. And at last she heard a soft footstep outside her door. As Julia watched, the door handle slowly turned.

But the door wouldn't open because of the desk in front. There was a pause, and then a quiet knock on the door. Julia held her breath. The knock came again – still quiet.

For a long time Julia sat there, nervous and wide awake – but no one knocked again. She finally fell asleep, and was woken early in the morning by the school bell.

After breakfast, when the girls went to different classrooms for their lessons, Julia managed to reach the wall surrounding the school without being seen. She climbed a large tree, sat on top of the wall, and then dropped down the other side. She knew that a bus was coming soon, and when it arrived she got on and went to the train station. There she got on the train to London.

Because so many girls had gone home and two teachers were dead, Julia thought it would be a while before anyone noticed she was gone. But just in case they were worried, she left a note in her bedroom for Miss Bulstrode, saying that she hadn't been kidnapped.

◆ ◆ ◆

Hercule Poirot was sitting in a room of his very modern flat when his personal servant, Georges, came to tell him he had a visitor.

'It's a young lady – a schoolgirl – who wants to see you urgently, sir,' said Georges. 'About some murders and a robbery.'

Poirot raised his eyebrows in surprise. 'Some murders, and a robbery? That is interesting. Show the young lady in.'

Julia came into the room and said politely, 'How do you do, Monsieur Poirot? My name is Julia Upjohn. A friend of my mother's has talked about you and said how clever you are. So when I couldn't decide what to do, I thought of you.'

'I am <u>honoured</u>,' said Poirot seriously. He brought Julia a chair and she sat down. 'Now tell me,' he said, 'about this robbery and these murders.'

'Miss Springer and Miss Vansittart have been murdered,' explained Julia. 'And there's the kidnapping, too – but I don't think that's really my business.'

'You confuse me,' said Poirot. 'Where have all these things occurred?'

'At my school – Meadowbank.'

'Ah!' Poirot exclaimed. 'At Meadowbank.' He picked up that day's newspaper and looked at the front page. 'I begin to understand,' he said. 'Now tell me everything, Mademoiselle Julia, from the beginning.'

Julia told him. It was a long story but she told it very clearly. At the end she described how she had looked inside the handle of the tennis racquet.

'And what was inside?' Poirot asked.

Julia lifted up her skirt, and quickly pulled off several pieces of sticky tape that held a small plastic wash bag to her leg. She opened the wash bag and suddenly poured the sparkling stones on to the table.

'My goodness!' exclaimed Poirot, in great surprise.

He picked up the jewels, letting them fall through his fingers. 'But they are real – genuine!'

Julia nodded. 'I think they are – that's why people have been killed.' She looked again at the jewels. 'But Monsieur Poirot, who do they belong to?'

'It is very difficult to know. But they do not belong to either you or to me. We must now decide what to do next.'

Hercule Poirot closed his eyes in thought. After a while he sat up. 'It seems that in this case I cannot remain in my chair. There must be order and method, but in what you tell me, there is no order and method. That is because we have here many different things that have been happening – but they all meet at Meadowbank. So I, too, go to Meadowbank. And as for you, Mademoiselle Julia – where is your mother?'

'Mummy's gone on a bus to Anatolia.'

'I see,' said Poirot. 'So instead we must tell your good head teacher that you are safe, and that I will bring you back to Meadowbank.'

'Miss Bulstrode knows I'm all right. I left a note saying I hadn't been kidnapped.'

'She will like to know for sure,' said Poirot, picking up the phone. Soon he was talking to Miss Bulstrode.

'Ah, Miss Bulstrode? My name is Hercule Poirot. I have with me here your pupil, Julia Upjohn. I am bringing her back in my car immediately, and will tell the local police that a certain valuable package is now safely in the bank.'

When he put down the phone, Julia said, 'But the jewels aren't in the bank.'

'They will be in a very short time,' said Poirot. 'But if anyone at Meadowbank was listening, or knows about the jewels, they now know that you do not have them any more. I said that to keep you safe, my child. I will admit that I have formed a high opinion of your courage and your intelligence.'

Julia looked pleased, but embarrassed.

CHAPTER 18

CONSULTATION

Miss Bulstrode had heard of Hercule Poirot and greeted him warmly. 'It was kind of you, Monsieur Poirot, to ring about Julia,' she said. 'Especially since with all the confusion here, we hadn't noticed she had gone. Perhaps it would have been better, Julia, to tell me what you were planning to do.'

'I didn't want to,' said Julia, 'in case someone heard me.'

'I'm not annoyed,' said Miss Bulstrode, 'but I would like to know exactly what's going on.'

'You permit?' said Hercule Poirot. He walked to the door, opened it and looked out, before shutting it very obviously. He returned, smiling widely.

'We are alone,' he said mysteriously. 'We can begin.'

Miss Bulstrode looked at the door and her eyebrows rose in surprise. She looked at Poirot and then slowly nodded her head. 'Now then, Julia,' she said. 'Tell me what's happened.'

Julia told her story again. When she finished, Hercule Poirot said, 'What Mademoiselle Julia found is now safely in the bank. It is hoped that no more unpleasant events will occur at Meadowbank.' He looked again towards the door.

'I think I understand,' said Miss Bulstrode.

'But it is important, Mademoiselle Julia, that you do not say anything about what you found, even to your friends,' added Poirot. 'Can you do that?'

'Yes,' said Julia. 'I won't tell anyone.'

Miss Bulstrode smiled. 'I hope your mother will be home soon,' she said. 'Inspector Kelsey tells me that they are trying hard to contact her – but buses in Anatolia are often delayed.'

'I can tell Mummy, can't I?' said Julia.

'Of course. Well, thank you, Julia,' Miss Bulstrode said. 'You'd better go to your class now.'

Julia left, closing the door behind her. Miss Bulstrode looked at Poirot. 'I think I understand,' she said again. 'You only pretended to shut the door – in fact you left it slightly open.'

Poirot nodded. 'Yes,' he said. 'If there was anyone who wanted to <u>overhear</u>, they now know that what Mademoiselle Julia found is in the bank. She should now be safe here.'

◆ ◆ ◆

Hercule Poirot was in a meeting with Inspector Kelsey and Adam Goodman.

'Now the jewels have been found,' Kelsey was saying, 'this is a very sensitive situation. Some very important people don't want any stories about the jewels in the newspapers. Officially it's best that we know nothing about them.'

'Yes,' agreed Hercule Poirot slowly. 'It is best to say nothing about the jewels. It is possible, after all, that they may still be hidden somewhere in Ramat.'

Inspector Kelsey sighed with relief. 'Thank you, Monsieur Poirot. <u>Unofficially</u>, these important people would like to leave the jewels with you.'

'I do not object,' said Poirot. 'Let us leave it at that. We have more serious things to think about, have we not? The jewels are valuable, but I say that human life is worth more.'

'You're right, Monsieur Poirot,' said Inspector Kelsey. 'We must catch this murderer. We'd be very interested to know what you think.'

'Then tell me, if you please,' said Poirot, 'all that is known so far.' He settled down to listen.

When Inspector Kelsey and Adam Goodman had told him everything, Hercule Poirot closed his eyes and slowly nodded his head. 'Let us start with the kidnapping of Princess Shaista,' he said. 'From what you have said, Inspector, it does not make much sense.'

'That's what I thought,' said Kelsey slowly. 'And though there have been ransom demands, they aren't genuine. No one has collected the ransom money.'

'So Princess Shaista was not kidnapped for ransom money, and it is clear that she did not know where the jewels were hidden. So there must be some other reason...'

He sat in silence, frowning, for a moment or two. Then he sat up, and asked a question. 'Her knees,' he said. 'Did you ever notice Princess Shaista's knees?'

Adam stared at him in astonishment.

'No,' he said. 'Why should I? The girls wear skirts most of the time, which cover their knees.'

'In the swimming pool, perhaps?' suggested Poirot hopefully.

'I never saw Shaista go swimming,' said Adam. 'I expect it was too cold for her. So what do you mean? Does she have a scar, or something like that?'

'No, no, that is not it at all. Ah well, instead I will contact my old friend, the Chief of Police in Switzerland. He may be able to help us.'

'Shaista was at school in Switzerland,' said Kelsey. 'Did anything happen there?'

'It is possible, yes,' said Poirot. He paused. 'But now we pass from kidnapping to something more serious. Murder.'

CHAPTER 19

CONSULTATION CONTINUED

'Two murders at Meadowbank,' said Poirot thoughtfully, 'in the Sports Pavilion. Now we know why. Because in the Sports Pavilion there was a tennis racquet containing a fortune in jewels.

'Someone knew about that racquet. Who was it? Was it Miss Springer herself? She did not like people going to the Sports Pavilion. She was angry with Mademoiselle Blanche.'

Poirot turned to Adam. 'And you say that Mademoiselle Blanche behaved strangely when she came out of the Sports Pavilion?'

'Yes,' said Adam. 'She didn't need to explain to me why she was there – but she told me anyway.'

Poirot nodded thoughtfully. 'And Miss Springer – why was she in the Sports Pavilion so late at night?' He turned to Kelsey. 'Where was Miss Springer before she came to Meadowbank?'

'We don't know,' said the Inspector. 'She left her previous job last summer, and we don't know where she's been since then. She has no close relatives or friends we can talk to.'

'So she could have been in Ramat,' said Poirot thoughtfully.

'I believe there were some schoolteachers in Ramat when the revolution started,' said Adam.

'Let us say, then,' suggested Poirot, 'that Miss Springer was in Ramat, and somehow learned that the jewels were in the tennis racquet. She waits until she knows the routine at Meadowbank, and then one night she goes to the Sports Pavilion to remove the jewels.'

He paused. 'Someone else had been watching her, followed her – and shot her. But they had no time to get the jewels or take the tennis racquet, because the shot was heard and people were quickly approaching the Sports Pavilion.'

'Do you think that's what happened?' asked Inspector Kelsey.

'I do not know,' said Poirot. 'It is one possibility. The other is that the person with the gun was already there, and was surprised by Miss Springer. Miss Springer was a nosey woman – perhaps she was suspicious of someone.'

'And who was the other person?' asked Adam.

'I do not know,' Poirot said again. 'You say you have checked most carefully everyone staying nearby. So it must be someone at Meadowbank.'

Kelsey sighed. 'Yes,' he agreed. 'Almost anyone could have killed Miss Springer – except Miss Johnson and Miss Chadwick. But the second murder narrows things down. Miss Rich, Miss Blake and Miss Shapland have good alibis.'

'And Miss Bulstrode?' Poirot asked. Adam smiled.

'She was staying with the Duchess of Welsham,' said Kelsey, 'so she too has an alibi. That leaves us with Miss Rowan and Mademoiselle Blanche. Miss Rowan has been here over a year and we have no reason to suspect her.'

'So we come back to Mademoiselle Blanche,' said Poirot.

There was a silence.

'There's no evidence against her,' said Kelsey. 'Her references seem genuine.'

'They would have to be,' said Poirot.

'Wait a minute,' said Kelsey. 'I remember that Mademoiselle Blanche said something about a key. She picked up the key to the Sports Pavilion and forgot to put it back. Miss Springer shouted at her.'

'To visit the Sports Pavilion at night you would need a key,' said Poirot. 'For that, it would have been necessary to make a copy of the key.'

'But why then would she tell you about the key?' asked Adam.

'In case Miss Springer had talked about it,' said Kelsey. 'But that doesn't help us much.' He looked gloomily at Poirot.

'But we must not forget,' said Poirot, 'that Julia Upjohn's mother recognized someone here at Meadowbank – a possible secret agent.'

'Yes, but we can't find Mrs Upjohn,' said Inspector Kelsey. 'She's not on a proper tour, she's travelling on local buses. She could be anywhere – Anatolia is a big place. So until we find her, we can't do anything – and Mademoiselle Blanche might walk out of Meadowbank at any time.'

Poirot shook his head. 'She will not do that,' he said. 'If you have committed murder, you do not draw attention to yourself.'

'I hope you're right,' Kelsey said.

'I am sure I am right,' said Poirot. 'And remember, the person whom Mrs Upjohn saw does not know that Mrs Upjohn saw her. The surprise when it comes will be complete.'

'It still doesn't help us much,' Kelsey sighed.

'There are other things,' Poirot added. 'Conversation, for example. Sooner or later, a person with something to hide says too much. Innocent people, also, know things without knowing they are important. And that reminds me—'

Poirot stood up. 'Excuse me,' he said. 'I must go and find someone who can draw.'

'Well,' said Adam, after Poirot went out. 'First girls' knees, and now drawing! I hope he knows what he's doing.'

◆ ◆ ◆

Miss Rich could draw well, and she sat down next to Poirot with a pencil and paper.

'Please, can you draw Miss Springer for me?' Poirot asked.

'That's difficult,' said Miss Rich. 'I didn't know her for very long. But I'll try.' She frowned for a moment and then began to draw quickly.

'*Bien*,' said Poirot, taking the drawing. 'Good. And now, if you please, can you draw Miss Bulstrode, Miss Rowan, Mademoiselle Blanche and – the gardener, Adam.'

Eileen Rich looked at him doubtfully, but then began to draw.

Poirot nodded. 'You are good,' he said. 'You can draw a good <u>likeness</u> with a few lines of the pencil. Now, can you change Miss Bulstrode's hair, and the shape of her eyebrows.'

Eileen stared at him for a while, and then did as he asked.

'Excellent,' said Poirot. 'Now do the same for Mademoiselle Blanche and Miss Rowan.'

When she had finished, he put the three drawings together.

'Now I will show you something,' he said. 'Miss Bulstrode, even with the changes you have made, still looks like Miss Bulstrode. But the other two, because they do not have Miss Bulstrode's strong personality, they appear almost different people, do they not?'

'I see what you mean,' said Eileen Rich. She watched Poirot put away the drawings carefully. 'What are you going to do with them?'

'Use them,' said Poirot.

CHAPTER 20

CONVERSATION

'Well,' said Mrs Sutcliffe doubtfully. 'I don't really know what to say.'

She looked at Hercule Poirot. 'It's been very upsetting,' she continued, 'and I'm glad to have Jennifer safely at home with me. Two murders and a girl kidnapped!'

'I would not worry too much about the kidnapping, Madame,' said Poirot. 'If I may tell you a secret, I suspect a romance.'

'Do you mean the girl just ran away to marry somebody?'

'I can say no more,' said Hercule Poirot. 'And I am sure that you too will say nothing of this.'

'Of course not,' said Mrs Sutcliffe, very pleased. She looked down at the letter that Poirot had brought from Inspector Kelsey. 'So Monsieur – er – Poirot, you want to talk to Jennifer? I'm afraid she's not a girl who notices things.' She called her daughter into the room.

'How do you do?' said Poirot. 'I am a friend of Julia Upjohn. She came to London to see me and ask my advice. She is now back at Meadowbank,' Poirot added.

Jennifer looked at her mother, annoyed. 'So *she* hasn't been taken away.' Mrs Sutcliffe decided to leave the room rather than argue again with her daughter.

'All this fuss!' said Jennifer. 'I told Mummy it was silly – no *pupils* have been killed. I wish I was back there.'

'I have come to ask, Mademoiselle Jennifer,' said Poirot, 'about the woman who came and gave you the new tennis racquet – what did she look like?'

'I don't really know,' said Jennifer. 'I didn't look at her much. She had blonde hair, and was wearing a blue dress and a big hat. I think she was American.'

'Had you ever seen her before?' asked Poirot.

'Oh no,' said Jennifer.

'Are you sure?' said Poirot. 'She was not, perhaps, one of the girls, dressed up – or one of the teachers?'

Jennifer looked puzzled. 'Dressed up?'

Poirot showed her the picture of Mademoiselle Blanche that Eileen Rich had drawn.

'Was this the woman?'

'It's a bit like her,' said Jennifer, 'but I don't think so. I didn't really look at her face.' She obviously didn't realize that the drawing was of Mademoiselle Blanche. 'I was looking at my new racquet.'

'I see,' said Poirot. After a pause, he asked, 'Did you ever see anyone at Meadowbank who you'd seen in Ramat?'

'In Ramat?' Jennifer thought. 'Oh no – at least – I don't think so.'

'But you are not sure, Mademoiselle Jennifer.'

'Well,' Jennifer looked worried. 'I often see people who look like other people,' she explained.

'Perhaps you recognized Princess Shaista?' suggested Poirot. 'You may have seen her in Ramat.'

'I don't think so,' said Jennifer, frowning. 'Of course I think most people do look alike. I only notice if someone has a strange sort of face, like Miss Rich.'

'Have you seen Miss Rich somewhere before?' Poirot asked.

'No,' said Jennifer. 'I think I saw someone who just looked like Miss Rich. This person was much fatter than she is.'

'Someone much fatter,' said Poirot thoughtfully.

'And Miss Rich was away ill last term,' added Jennifer. 'So she couldn't have been in Ramat.'

'And the other girls?' asked Poirot, 'had you seen any of the girls before?'

'Only the ones I knew already,' said Jennifer. 'But I don't really notice people very much.'

CHAPTER 21

GATHERING <u>THREADS</u>[7]

'I want to talk to you, Eileen,' said Miss Bulstrode.

Eileen Rich followed Miss Bulstrode into the sitting room. Meadowbank was strangely quiet. There weren't many pupils left and the teachers didn't have much to do. Miss Johnson didn't like having so much free time; Miss Chadwick wandered round looking very unhappy, while Ann Shapland did a lot of gardening – working closely with Adam…

'I want to talk to you about Meadowbank,' said Miss Bulstrode. 'The school may be ruined – perhaps no one will come back.'

'No,' interrupted Eileen Rich. 'You mustn't let that happen. It would be wrong.' She almost shouted with passion. 'Meadowbank is a great school, and it *must* be saved.'

'I promise that I'll do all I can,' said Miss Bulstrode. 'But what I want to say is this – if Meadowbank survives I want you to be the next head teacher.'

'Me?' Eileen Rich stared at her. '*Me?*'

'Yes, my dear,' said Miss Bulstrode. 'You.'

'I can't,' said Eileen Rich. 'I'm too young. I don't have enough experience.'

'You are the person I want to run this school when I retire,' said Miss Bulstrode firmly.

'But I thought – we all thought – that Miss Vansittart…'

'I did consider her very carefully for a long time,' admitted Miss Bulstrode. 'I'm sure everyone else thought Miss Vansittart would be the next head teacher. But I never said anything definite to her, and finally I decided she was not the person I wanted. I want someone with new ideas, who will think about the future. That's why I want you.'

'It would have been wonderful,' said Eileen Rich. 'Wonderful. But I really don't think I can – now. Perhaps I can think about it, Miss Bulstrode? I don't really know what to say.'

◆ ◆ ◆

'Miss Rich's hair is always so untidy,' remarked Ann Shapland, looking up from her gardening as the teacher walked by. 'Why doesn't she cut it all off?'

'You should suggest it to her,' said Adam.

'I don't know her that well,' said Ann Shapland. She paused. 'Do you think that Meadowbank will be able to continue?'

'I don't know,' said Adam. 'Will you come back next term if it does?'

'No,' said Ann firmly. 'I've had enough of schools and working with women. And I don't like murder. I think I'll marry Dennis and settle down.'

'Dennis?' said Adam. 'You told me about him. I think you can do better.'

'Are you making me an offer?' said Ann.

'Certainly not,' said Adam. 'And you wouldn't like to marry a gardener.'

'I was wondering about marrying a secret agent,' said Ann.

'I'm not a secret agent,' said Adam.

'No, no, of course not,' said Ann. 'You're not a secret agent, Shaista wasn't kidnapped – everything's fine. I've heard that Shaista has been found in Switzerland,' she added. 'How did she get there?'

'I've no idea,' said Adam. 'It was Monsieur Hercule Poirot who found her.'

'Is he the funny little man who brought Julia Upjohn back from London?' asked Ann.

'Yes, that's him,' said Adam. 'He went to see my mother,' he added. 'And Jennifer Sutcliffe's mother. He seems to be fascinated with people's mothers.'

'Did he go and see Miss Rich's mother, and Chaddy's?' said Ann. 'Poor Miss Chadwick – look, here she comes now.' She watched Miss Chadwick's approach. 'She looks much older since Miss Vansittart's death. She really loves Meadowbank. I'll go and talk to her.'

Ann went to meet Miss Chadwick and together they walked back to the house.

'It's so quiet here now,' said Ann, looking round.

'It's awful,' said Miss Chadwick, 'awful! I can't get over it. I can't sleep at night. Meadowbank is ruined – after all those years of work.'

'It may be all right,' said Ann. 'People will soon forget about the murders.'

'But not quickly enough,' said Miss Chadwick grimly. 'Not quickly enough.'

◆ ◆ ◆

Mademoiselle Blanche came out of the classroom at the end of her French lesson. She looked at her watch. Yes, she did have enough time.

She went upstairs to her room and got ready to go out. As she looked at herself in the mirror, she smiled. Sometimes it was good to be a person who no one noticed. It made it easy for her to use her sister Angèle's references – and even her passport. Angèle was dead, but she had enjoyed teaching and was very good at it. She herself found it very boring.

But she wasn't going to be a teacher for much longer. She was going to have money.

Mademoiselle Blanche picked up her handbag and went out of the house, through the front gate to the bus stop. When the bus arrived she got on, and a quarter of an hour later she got out in the nearest big town. She went to a large department store and began to look at dresses.

After a while she went upstairs to the Ladies' rest room and found a telephone. No one was near enough to overhear her. She called a number and waited to hear if the right voice answered. It did.

'You know who I am?' she said. 'Yes. I am speaking of some money that you owe. You have until tomorrow evening to pay this money into this bank account.' She gave the details. 'If not, I will tell the police what I saw on the night that Miss Springer died.' She put down the phone.

After doing a little shopping, Mademoiselle Blanche took the bus back to Meadowbank. She smiled to herself. She had asked for money, but not too much. The money would last for a while – and then she would ask for more. Life was going to be very pleasant in the future.

Back at Meadowbank Mademoiselle Blanche walked past the swimming pool, and watched Eileen Rich and Ann Shapland swimming and diving with the girls in the pool. She was in time for her afternoon classes. During her lesson the girls talked and didn't listen to her, but she hardly noticed. She wasn't going to be a teacher for much longer.

When the bell rang, Mademoiselle Blanche went upstairs to her room to tidy her hair before dinner. But, as she looked in the mirror, she saw a sudden movement behind her – so quick that she was completely surprised. As Mademoiselle Blanche opened her mouth to scream, a sandbag hit her silently on the back of her neck.

CHAPTER 22

INCIDENT IN ANATOLIA

Mrs Upjohn was sitting by the side of a road somewhere in Anatolia. She and a large Turkish woman were talking, partly in French and partly by using their hands. The other passengers were sitting nearby, watching the bus driver trying to start the broken-down bus. Mrs Upjohn's journey had also been delayed by heavy rain and blocked roads.

'Mrs Upjohn?' said a very British voice, which didn't sound as if it belonged in Anatolia.

Mrs Upjohn looked up. She hadn't noticed that a car had arrived, and an obviously British man had got out.

'Mrs Upjohn,' the man said again. 'My name's Derek O'Connor, from the British Government. We've been trying to contact you for days.'

'Contact me? Why? Is it Julia?' Mrs Upjohn said sharply. 'Has something happened to Julia?'

'No, no,' said O'Connor. 'Julia is all right. No, there's been some trouble at Meadowbank and we want to take you there as soon as possible. I'll drive you back to the nearest airport, and you can get on a plane in a few hours.'

Mrs Upjohn opened her mouth and then shut it again. She stood up, collected her luggage and said goodbye to the Turkish woman. She followed O'Connor to his car without asking any questions.

O'Connor thought that Mrs Upjohn was a very sensible woman.

CHAPTER 23

SHOWDOWN

Miss Bulstrode looked around at her staff, who were all sitting together in one of the school classrooms. Miss Chadwick was there, and Miss Johnson, Miss Rich, Miss Rowan and Miss Blake. Ann Shapland sat with her notebook and pencil, ready to take notes. Hercule Poirot and Detective Inspector Kelsey sat beside Miss Bulstrode, while Adam Goodman sat slightly behind them.

Miss Bulstrode stood up. 'As you all work here,' she said, 'I thought you'd like to know exactly what is known about the recent unfortunate events at Meadowbank. Detective Inspector Kelsey is not allowed to give us any official police information, but Monsieur Hercule Poirot, the well-known detective, will now tell you what he has discovered.'

Hercule Poirot rose to his feet, smiled widely at his audience and carefully smoothed his moustache. 'I know that this has been a difficult time for you all,' he began. 'You have lost three of your colleagues — Miss Springer, Miss Vansittart and Mademoiselle Blanche. This is because Meadowbank has become the centre of certain events. And also because there is someone here who does not belong.' He looked around the room. 'There is a cat among the pigeons.

'But before I talk about the murders, I will deal first with the kidnapping.' He took a photograph from his pocket and passed it round so all the people in the room saw it.

'Do you recognize the girl in this photograph?' Poirot asked.

Everyone shook their heads.

'Ah, but you should,' said Poirot, 'since this is a photograph, from Switzerland, of Princess Shaista.'

'But that's not Shaista,' said Miss Chadwick.

'Exactly,' said Poirot. 'This story starts in Ramat, where three months ago there was a revolution. The ruler, Prince Ali Yusuf, died trying to escape, but some very valuable jewels that he owned were not found in the wreckage of his plane. Several groups of people wanted to find them. They thought that the jewels might be brought to Princess Shaista, the prince's cousin and only close relative.

'It was known that Princess Shaista was coming to school at Meadowbank. However, the girl's uncle, the Emir Ibrahim, was abroad and Miss Bulstrode did not know Shaista personally. Shaista was indeed kidnapped – but not from Meadowbank. She was in fact kidnapped before she even arrived here.

'It was a simple plan,' explained Poirot. 'The real Shaista is in fact still in Switzerland, and has now been found. Instead it was a secret agent, hoping to hear news of the jewels, who arrived in London and was brought to Meadowbank.

'But the false Shaista – a young French actress – was obviously older than the real Shaista. I did ask,' said Hercule Poirot thoughtfully, 'if anyone had noticed Shaista's knees. The knees of a woman of twenty-four can never really be mistaken for the knees of a girl of fifteen. Nobody, <u>alas</u>, had noticed her knees.

'But nobody tried to contact the false Shaista about the jewels, and when Miss Springer was murdered it was feared that Shaista's uncle, the Emir Ibrahim, would come to England. The false Shaista began to talk about kidnapping, and when the Emir did arrive, she was indeed "kidnapped". In fact the car that came early to collect her left her in the nearest town, and she simply went back to using her own identity. A false ransom note was sent to make the kidnapping story appear real. It does not occur to anyone that the kidnapping really occurred earlier in Switzerland.'

Poirot meant, of course, that it had not occurred to anyone but himself!

'We pass now,' he continued, 'to something far more serious – murder.

'The false Shaista was at Meadowbank just to hear about the jewels. She had no motive for murder, and although she could have killed Miss Springer, she could not have killed Miss Vansittart or Mademoiselle Blanche.

'Let us go back now to Ramat where all this started. Prince Ali Yusuf gave the jewels to his pilot, Bob Rawlinson. Bob Rawlinson visited his sister, Mrs Sutcliffe, in her hotel in Ramat, and stayed in her room for twenty minutes, even though she was not there. Several different groups of people guessed that Bob Rawlinson had hidden the jewels somewhere in his sister's luggage. One group of people did not know where, and searched Mrs Sutcliffe's luggage and burgled her house. But someone else definitely knew where the jewels were hidden – in the handle of the tennis racquet belonging to Mrs Sutcliffe's daughter, Jennifer.

'This person went out to the Sports Pavilion one night, having previously made a copy of the key, to look at the tennis racquets. But Miss Springer saw a light in the Sports Pavilion and went out to investigate. Discovered and recognized by Miss Springer, the killer did not hesitate... Miss Springer was shot dead. But the shot had been heard, and the crime was discovered almost immediately. The murderer had to escape quickly, leaving the tennis racquet behind.

'A few days later a strange woman with an American accent spoke to Jennifer Sutcliffe and gave her a new tennis racquet, taking the old one away. But the woman did not know that Jennifer Sutcliffe and Julia Upjohn had swapped racquets, so the racquet that she took away was really Julia Upjohn's old racquet.

'We come now to the second murder,' continued Poirot. 'Miss Vansittart was looking at Shaista's locker – probably looking for a clue to the girl's disappearance. Someone followed her, and killed her with a sandbag. Again the crime was discovered almost immediately – by Miss Chadwick.

'The police again took charge of the Sports Pavilion, and again the killer had no opportunity to look at the tennis racquets. But by now, Julia Upjohn, an intelligent child, had realized that her racquet – which had belonged to Jennifer – was important. She looked inside the handle and found the jewels. These she brought to me, and they are now safely in the bank.'

Poirot paused. 'As to the third murder, Mademoiselle Blanche knew – we do not know how – who the murderer was. She did not tell the police, but instead she asked the murderer for money to keep silent – <u>blackmail</u>. But there is nothing more dangerous than blackmailing a person who has killed perhaps twice already – and Mademoiselle Blanche too, was killed.'

Hercule Poirot paused again. 'So that,' he said, looking around 'is the account of this whole affair.'

They were all staring at him, and their faces now showed no emotion.

'Though of course,' added Poirot, 'Inspector Kelsey, Adam Goodman and I have been making inquiries. We have to know, you see, if there is still a cat among the pigeons!

'I am happy to say that everyone here is indeed who they say they are. So we are not looking for someone pretending to be someone else. The murderer is someone using their real identity.'

Everyone was very still now. There was a feeling of danger in the air.

'We are looking,' continued Poirot, 'for someone who was in Ramat three months ago, and who saw Bob Rawlinson hide the jewels in the tennis racquet. Miss Chadwick was here at Meadowbank, Miss Johnson was here, and so were Miss Rowan and Miss Blake.'

He pointed his finger. 'But Miss Rich – Miss Rich was not here last term, was she?'

'I – no. I was ill.' She spoke quickly. 'I was away for a term.'

'So you could have been in Ramat,' said Poirot. 'I think you were. We can look at your passport.'

There was a moment's silence, then Eileen Rich looked up. 'Yes,' she said quietly. 'I was in Ramat. I was ill and my doctor advised me to go abroad to rest.'

'That is true,' said Miss Bulstrode. 'I received a doctor's certificate saying that Miss Rich needed to rest for a term.'

'So – you went to Ramat?' said Hercule Poirot.

'Why shouldn't I go to Ramat?' Eileen Rich's voice shook a little. 'I wanted a rest and sunshine. I was there for two months.'

'There you were recognized,' said Poirot, 'by Jennifer Sutcliffe. She thought she saw you in Ramat, but said that the person she saw was fat, not thin.'

'What are you trying to say?' said Miss Rich. 'That I murdered these people? It isn't true, I tell you. It isn't true!'

'Inspector Kelsey?' Poirot turned his head.

Inspector Kelsey nodded. He went to the door, opened it, and Mrs Upjohn walked into the room.

◆ ◆ ◆

'Mrs Upjohn,' said Hercule Poirot into the silence. 'We would like to ask you something. When you brought your daughter Julia to Meadowbank you looked out of the window of Miss Bulstrode's sitting room and recognized someone, did you not?'

Mrs Upjohn stared at him. 'Yes, I did see someone,' she said. 'Someone I hadn't seen for years. I wondered what she was doing here.'

'Mrs Upjohn,' said Inspector Kelsey. 'Will you look round this room and tell me if you see that person here now?'

'Yes, of course,' said Mrs Upjohn. 'I saw her as soon as I came in. That's her.'

She pointed her finger. Inspector Kelsey was quick and so was Adam, but they were not quick enough. Ann Shapland had jumped up and was pointing a gun straight at Mrs Upjohn. Miss Bulstrode moved forward quickly and stood in front of Mrs Upjohn, but Miss Chadwick was even quicker.

'No, you won't!' cried Miss Chadwick, and threw her body in front of Miss Bulstrode just as the gun was fired. Miss Chadwick slowly fell to the floor as Adam and Kelsey took hold of the struggling Ann Shapland, and took the gun away from her.

'They said then that she was a killer,' said Mrs Upjohn breathlessly. 'She was one of the most dangerous young agents they had.'

'You liar!' Ann Shapland shouted angrily.

'She does not lie,' said Hercule Poirot. 'You *are* dangerous. Until now you have never been suspected when you have used your own identity. You have taken real jobs using your own name – all to gain information. You have worked at an oil company, with an archaeologist whose work took him all around the world, and an important government minister. Ever since you were seventeen you have worked as a secret agent for many different people, and for a great deal of money. In most of your jobs you have used your own name, though for others you used a different identity. At those times you said you went home to look after your mother.

'But I strongly suspect, Miss Shapland, that the elderly woman I visited is not your real mother. This genuine mental patient with a confused mind is your excuse for leaving your jobs. You did not spend three months this year with your "mother" – instead you went to Ramat. Not as Ann Shapland, but as Angelica de Toredo, a Spanish dancer. From your hotel room you somehow saw Bob Rawlinson hide the jewels in the tennis racquet.

'You could not take them then because the British people left Ramat suddenly because of the revolution. Instead you read the luggage labels and found out that Jennifer Sutcliffe was going to school at Meadowbank. I have discovered that you paid Miss Bulstrode's secretary a large amount of money to leave her job – and you took her place.

'One night you went to the Sports Pavilion to find the jewels,' Poirot said. 'But Miss Springer saw you and followed you – and you shot her. Later, Mademoiselle Blanche tried to blackmail you, and you killed her, too. It comes naturally to you, does it not, to kill?'

He stopped. Inspector Kelsey stepped forward and officially arrested Ann Shapland, who swore and struggled wildly as she was taken out of the room.

Miss Johnson was kneeling by Miss Chadwick. 'I'm afraid she's badly hurt,' she said. 'We need a doctor, immediately!'

Chapter 24

Poirot explains

'You did it very well, Monsieur Poirot,' said Inspector Kelsey. 'You made Ann Shapland think that we were going to arrest Miss Rich, and Mrs Upjohn's sudden appearance completely surprised her. If the bullet in that gun matches the one that killed Miss Springer...'

'It will, my friend, it will,' said Poirot.

'Then we'll have definite evidence that Ann Shapland murdered Miss Springer. And of course she shot Miss Chadwick. But I still don't understand how she killed Miss Vansittart. It's impossible – she has a perfect alibi.'

'It is true,' Poirot said, 'that Ann Shapland killed Miss Springer and Mademoiselle Blanche. But Miss Vansittart...' He hesitated for a moment, and looked at Miss Bulstrode. 'Miss Vansittart was killed by Miss Chadwick.'

'Miss Chadwick?' exclaimed Miss Bulstrode and Kelsey together.

Poirot nodded. 'I am sure of it.'

'But – but why?' said Miss Bulstrode.

'I think,' explained Poirot, 'that Miss Chadwick loved Meadowbank too much. When you retired she wanted to be the next head teacher.'

'But she's much too old,' said Miss Bulstrode.

'Yes,' said Poirot, 'but she didn't think so. Then she found out that you were thinking of making Eleanor Vansittart head teacher. Miss Chadwick loved Meadowbank, and she did not like Eleanor Vansittart. I think in the end she hated her. She was jealous.'

'I see…' said Miss Bulstrode slowly. 'Yes, yes, I see… I should have known.'

'And when you went away for the weekend you chose Eleanor Vansittart to be in charge…' said Poirot gently. 'This is what I think happened. Just as she said, Miss Chadwick saw the light in the Sports Pavilion and went out to investigate. But it was Miss Vansittart who took a golf club with her – not Miss Chadwick. Miss Chadwick took a sandbag, and when she saw Eleanor Vansittart kneeling down she lifted the sandbag and hit her.

'Miss Chadwick was <u>horrified</u> by what she had done – she had killed Miss Vansittart because she was jealous. But now she was sure she would be the next head teacher, so she told the police that she had taken the golf club, not the sandbag – which she put back.'

'But why did Ann Shapland kill Mademoiselle Blanche with a sandbag?' asked Miss Bulstrode.

'Because she could not use her gun, as the shot would be heard,' explained Poirot. 'And she cleverly wanted to connect the third murder with the second one – because for the second murder she had an alibi.'

'And why did you ask Eileen Rich to draw various members of my staff?'

'I wanted to see if Jennifer Sutcliffe would recognize a face. But she did not recognize Mademoiselle Blanche with a different hairstyle, so it is doubtful that she would have recognized Ann Shapland.'

'So was Ann Shapland the woman with the racquet?' asked Miss Bulstrode.

'Yes,' said Poirot. 'All this time she has been working alone – to get the jewels for herself. That day you rang your buzzer to ask for Mademoiselle Julia, Ann Shapland did not answer. She put on a blonde <u>wig</u> and a blue dress, and was away from her desk for only twenty minutes.'

'And Miss Rich?' Miss Bulstrode looked thoughtful.

Hercule Poirot and Inspector Kelsey looked at each other. 'Talk to her,' said Poirot, as the two men left the room. 'That is the best thing to do.'

When Eileen Rich appeared, her face was white. 'So you want to know what I was doing in Ramat?'

'I think I know,' said Miss Bulstrode. 'Jennifer said you were fat. She didn't realize you were pregnant.'

'Yes,' said Eileen Rich. 'I was going to have a baby. I didn't want to lose my job here, so when I couldn't hide it any longer I said I was ill and went abroad to Ramat. But my baby – my baby was born dead. I came back this term and hoped that no one would ever know. That's why I had to say no when you asked me to be the next head teacher.'

She paused and said calmly, 'Would you like me to leave now? Or wait until the end of term?'

'I want you to stay – and come back next term,' said Miss Bulstrode, 'if there is one.'

'Come back?' said Eileen Rich. 'Do you mean you still want me?'

'Of course I do,' said Miss Bulstrode. 'You haven't murdered anyone, have you? You had a love affair and a baby. But I think the real passion of your life is teaching.'

'Oh yes,' agreed Eileen Rich. 'I love teaching more than anything else!'

'You're a fine teacher,' said Miss Bulstrode. 'Together we'll work hard to make Meadowbank successful again – and we'll do it.'

'It'll be the best school in England,' said Eileen Rich with excitement. 'Yes, I'll stay.'

'Good,' said Miss Bulstrode, 'And Eileen, please go and get your hair cut properly. But now,' she said, her voice changing, 'I must go to Chaddy.'

♦ ◆ ♦

Miss Chadwick was lying in bed, very white and still. Miss Johnson and a policeman with a notebook sat nearby.

'Hello, Chaddy,' said Miss Bulstrode, taking her hand. Miss Chadwick's eyes opened.

'I want to tell you,' she said. 'Eleanor – it was – it was me.'

'Yes, dear, I know,' said Miss Bulstrode.

Tears fell slowly down Miss Chadwick's cheeks. 'It's so awful... I didn't mean to do it. I was jealous. I'll never forgive myself.'

'But you saved my life,' said Miss Bulstrode, 'and you saved Mrs Upjohn. That matters too, doesn't it?'

'I only wish,' said Miss Chadwick, 'I could give my life for you both. Then it would be all right...'

Miss Bulstrode looked at her with great pity. Miss Chadwick took a deep breath and smiled. Her head moved slightly to one side, and she died...

'You did give your life, my dear,' said Miss Bulstrode softly. 'I hope you realize that now.'

CHAPTER 25

LEGACY

'Mr Robinson is here to see you, sir,' said Georges.

'Ah!' said Hercule Poirot. He had received a letter from his friend Colonel Pikeaway about Mr Robinson. 'Show him in, Georges.'

Mr Robinson came into the room, bowed and shook hands politely. When he sat down he wiped his large yellow face with a handkerchief.

'I was interested to hear, Monsieur Poirot,' said Mr Robinson, 'of your involvement in the affairs of a girls' school – Meadowbank. I hear too that three murders were committed by an unfortunate young woman – a young woman who violently hated schoolteachers...'

'No doubt,' said Poirot <u>dryly</u>, 'that is what her <u>defence lawyer</u> will say.'

'She was good at her job, I believe,' sighed Mr Robinson. 'Young, but very useful – to many different people. But it was a mistake for her to work alone, and try to take the jewels for herself.'

Poirot nodded.

Mr Robinson leaned forward. 'I have come to ask where the jewels are now, Monsieur Poirot.' he asked. 'And what are you going to do with them?'

'I have been waiting for suggestions,' said Poirot. 'They do not belong to me, and I would like to give them to their true owner.'

'And I am here to suggest that you give the jewels to me,' said Mr Robinson.

'Ah,' said Poirot. 'And why should I do that?'

'Because they were the personal property of the late Prince Ali Yusuf, who told his friend Bob Rawlinson to get them out of Ramat. If he succeeded, he was supposed to give the jewels to me.'

'Have you proof of that?'

'Certainly.' Mr Robinson handed him a large envelope, and Poirot read the papers inside very carefully. 'It seems to be as you say,' he said. 'May I ask what you, personally, get for doing this?'

Mr Robinson looked surprised. 'Money, of course,' he said. 'A large amount of money. There are many people like me in the world. We arrange financial matters for important people – kings, presidents, princes. We charge a lot of money for our services, but we are honest.'

'I see,' said Poirot. '*Eh bien*! I agree to what you ask. But I am curious. What are you going to do with the jewels?'

Mr Robinson looked at Hercule Poirot. His large face smiled as he told Poirot his plans.

◆ ◆ ◆

Children were playing and running in the street. One of them bumped into Mr Robinson as he stepped out of his expensive car.

Mr Robinson opened the gate to number 15, and knocked on the door of the neat little house. The door was opened by a fair, pleasant-looking girl of about twenty-five.

'Mr Robinson?' she said with a smile. 'I got your letter. Please come in.' She led him into a small sitting room. 'Would you like some tea?' she asked.

'Thank you, but no. I can only stay a short time. As I said in my letter, I have come to bring you something.'

'From Ali?'

'Yes.'

'So there isn't – any hope? I mean – it's true? He's really dead?'

'I'm afraid so,' said Mr Robinson gently.

'I didn't really expect to see him again when he went back to Ramat,' said the girl. 'I knew he had to stay there, and marry one of his own people.'

Mr Robinson took out a package and put it on the table. 'Open it, please.'

She opened the package, and breathed in quickly as she saw the beautiful, bright jewels inside. 'Are they – are they real?'

'They are real,' said Mr Robinson. 'They are worth about one million pounds.'

'I can't believe it.' She wrapped the jewels up again, just as the door burst open and a small boy rushed in. 'Mum, look! Look at this. I –' He stopped, staring at Mr Robinson. The boy had dark hair and dark skin.

'Go into the kitchen, Allen,' said his mother. 'Your dinner's ready.'

'Oh good.' He hurried out again.

'You call him Allen?' said Mr Robinson.

'It was the nearest name to Ali. It would have been difficult for him to be named after his father.' She paused. 'What am I going to do?'

'First, I need to see your marriage certificate,' said Mr Robinson. 'Hmm, yes,' he said, when she gave it to him. 'Ali Yusuf... married to... Alice Calder... Yes, this is all perfectly legal.'

'No one knew who he was,' said Alice. 'I was pregnant with Allen, and Ali said we should be married. It was all he could do for me. He did love me. We always knew he would have to leave, but he did love me.'

'Yes,' said Mr Robinson. 'I'm sure he did. Now,' he continued, 'I can sell these jewels for you and get you a good lawyer to take care of your affairs. You're going to be a very rich woman.'

'Yes, all right,' she said, giving him the jewels. 'Take them. But I'd like to give one to the schoolgirl who found them. A green one, perhaps.'

'An excellent idea,' said Mr Robinson. He stood up. 'I shall charge you a lot of money,' he said, 'but I won't cheat you.'

She looked at him calmly. 'No, I don't think you will. And I need someone who knows about business.'

'You seem to be a very sensible woman,' said Mr Robinson. 'Now I will take the jewels. Are you sure you don't want to keep one for yourself?'

'No,' said Alice slowly. 'I won't keep... even one. I don't need jewels to remember Ali. I have Allen.'

'A most unusual woman,' said Robinson to himself as he walked out to his car. 'Yes, a most unusual woman...'

◆ CHARACTER LIST ◆

Miss Honoria Bulstrode: the co-founder and head teacher

Miss Chadwick (also called 'Chaddy'): the co-founder and Mathematics teacher

Miss Eleanor Vansittart: the History and German teacher

Ann Shapland: Miss Bulstrode's new secretary

Dennis Rathbone: a friend of Ann Shapland, who wants to marry her

Miss Johnson: the school matron

Mademoiselle Angèle Blanche: the new French teacher

Miss Eileen Rich: the English and Geography teacher

Miss Elspeth Rowan: a junior teacher

Miss Blake: a junior teacher

Princess Shaista: the cousin of Prince Ali Yusuf of Ramat, and a new pupil at Meadowbank school

Mrs Upjohn: Julia Upjohn's mother; in the war she worked with secret agents

Julia Upjohn: Mrs Upjohn's daughter, a friend of Jennifer Sutcliffe, and a pupil at Meadowbank school

Lady Veronica Carlton: a visiting parent at Meadowbank school

Prince Ali Yusuf: the Sheikh and ruler of Ramat, a fictional, small, but very rich, country in the Middle East

Bob Rawlinson: the friend and pilot of Prince Ali Yusuf, and the brother of Joan Sutcliffe

Achmed: works with Bob as a senior mechanic at the airport in Ramat

Mrs Joan Sutcliffe: Jennifer's mother and Bob Rawlinson's sister

John Edmundson: works at the British Embassy in Ramat, and a friend of Bob Rawlinson

Jennifer Sutcliffe: daughter of Joan and Henry, niece of Bob Rawlinson, and a pupil at Meadowbank school

Colonel Pikeaway: works for the Secret Service of the British Government

Adam Goodman: a secret agent for the British Government, sent to watch Princess Shaista while pretending to be the new gardener

Mr Robinson: an important international financier

Señora Angelica de Toredo: a Spanish dancer

Derek O'Connor: works for the Secret Service of the British Government

Andrew Ball: a thief who broke into the Sutcliffe house

Henry Sutcliffe: married to Joan Sutcliffe, and father of Jennifer

Miss Grace Springer: the new Games teacher

Mr Briggs: the old gardener

Detective Inspector Kelsey: the police officer in charge of the murder investigation

Emir Ibrahim: Princess Shaista's uncle

Mrs Gina Campbell: Jennifer Sutcliffe's aunt

Hercule Poirot: the famous Belgian detective

Georges: the personal servant of Hercule Poirot

Alice Calder: Allen's mother

Allen: son of Alice Calder

◆ Cultural notes ◆

1. Boarding schools in the 1950s

Boarding schools like 'Meadowbank', where students could live as well as study, were a popular alternative to the usual 'day schools' for richer parents, and they still exist today. In the past, most of these schools – just like Meadowbank – were 'single-sex': the students were either all boys, or all girls. Nowadays, many of them are mixed.

Agatha Christie actually never went to a school at all; she was taught at home instead. She had experience of boarding schools, however, because her sister went to one, and then later she sent her own daughter to one. Meadowbank is a fairly typical 1950s English boarding school.

The head teacher, Miss Bulstrode, who started the school with Miss Chadwick, has strong ideas about education. She wants her school to encourage the students to be individuals, each girl can decide what she is interested in, and the teachers will help her to do well in these subjects. Although the students usually take national or international tests and examinations before they graduate, the school is 'independent' and can choose what it teaches. It is the head teacher who decides which subjects are taught at the school, and she also chooses the teachers who will teach the classes. She is an important reason why parents choose a particular school for their children, and that is why everyone is so concerned about who should be the next head teacher at Meadowbank.

The school is an impressive place in the countryside, surrounded by beautiful gardens. Girls have their own rooms, and the matron's job is to make sure that they are happy and safe in their rooms. Miss Bulstrode believes sports are important in education, and the girls play typical school sports such as tennis and hockey. In British schools it is still common to call the sports lessons 'Games', and so Miss

Springer is called the Games teacher. The students at Meadowbank also have a swimming pool, and are very proud of their new Sports Pavillion where all of the modern sports equipment is kept. This makes the school an expensive place to study, but a place that people feel proud to belong to.

Most boarding schools have three terms, with long breaks for Christmas, Easter and summer. Important events in the story happen at the end of the third week of term, when students and the staff have a two-day vacation. While some boarding schools also have students who go home at night, all the pupils at Meadowbank live in the school 24 hours a day during term time.

The staff and teachers of boarding schools usually also live in the school, just like the students. In the 1950s, discipline was very strong, even for teachers and other staff, and so Ann Shapland says she can only leave the school when she has 'time off', just like the girls. The school is the centre of everyone's life during term time: your friends live there, you eat there, you work or study there, and you spend your free time there. (Many boarding schools even have their own special school vocabulary and traditions.)

2. British society, social 'class', and schools

This novel first appeared in 1959, when British society was still very conservative and traditional. Social 'class' – a person's 'place' in society – was very important and this depended mainly on your family background, and partly on your job. Meadowbank's important place in society is clear from the people who Miss Bulstrode knows – for example, she stays with a duchess during the vacation weekend. In British society, a duchess is only one step away in importance from the King or Queen.

Because Meadowbank was such a good school, it was very expensive. Many of the parents were very rich and important people. Students – or pupils, as they are often called in the UK – had the chance to make friends with the children of kings, queens, emirs, dukes and duchesses, lords and ladies, and important business people. This was another reason why parents might choose a school like Meadowbank, as these friendships could help their children in the future. Even today in the UK, some of the most important and famous people have been to boarding schools, although this is less true than it was before. Some of the oldest and best boarding schools today are still very famous.

The opinions of important people in society were extremely valuable to Meadowbank and to the parents of its students, but this means that any scandals could also easily destroy the school. A murder would start a big scandal, of course, but other, more private things could also shock society.

3. Secret Service

Adam Goodman is an important character in the story, but we never find out his real name. We know that he is working in an unnamed office in London, and that his boss – an army Colonel – can call people from the British Embassy to help him. We can guess that he must work for the British 'Secret Service'. His job is to protect his country, but unlike a soldier or a police officer, he has to do it secretly, sometimes outside of the law.

This story happens after the end of World War II, during which some men and women left their regular jobs and did dangerous work as secret agents to try to find out what the enemy was planning.

The Secret Service becomes involved in the story because of the political problems in the country of Ramat, where a group of people want to get rid of Prince Ali Yusuf's family, and become the new government. The British Government, through the British Embassy in Ramat, is responsible for the safety of the British people visiting or living in Ramat. The staff at the Embassy have to help these people escape the country quickly when the revolution begins. Agatha Christie invented Ramat, but she visited the Middle East many times, and was familiar with life for European 'expatriates' (people living outside of their own countries), and with British Embassies.

4. Straws in the wind

'Straw' here is 'dry grass' – something small and unimportant – but if you throw it into the air, it can tell you the direction of the wind, and that can perhaps tell you if a serious storm is coming. That's what this saying means: 'small signs that help you guess what will happen in the future'.

5. Cat among the pigeons

'Well, that's really put the cat among the pigeons!' is something you can hear people in the UK say today. They usually look worried when they say it, because it means that something has just happened that will cause big problems. Many people think that pigeons – a common bird in cities all over the world – are a problem, but a long time ago it was popular for people to keep pigeons as an important source of food. Unfortunately, pigeons are also very popular with cats. If a cat got into the cage, it could happily eat the birds one by one, and there was nothing the birds could do to protect themselves. If the pigeons in *this* story are the students and teachers at Meadowbank, then the question is: who is the cat...?

6. Aladdin

Aladdin is the hero of a famous traditional story from the Middle East, that has been told many times in books, plays and movies. At the beginning of the story, Aladdin is a poor boy who is sent by a strange man to find an old lamp in a mysterious cave. The man tricks the boy, and Aladdin becomes trapped in the cave, but he discovers that the lamp can do magic. He uses it to escape, and becomes very rich. He even marries the King's daughter, but he doesn't tell anyone his secret. One day, the strange man returns, and tries to get the lamp back by tricking Aladdin's wife. He pretends to be an old man in the street who exchanges 'new lamps for old ones' – you give him your old lamp, and he will give you a new one. Because Aladdin didn't tell his wife about his secret, she thinks the magic lamp is just a dirty old thing, and gives it to the old man. Eventually, using a magic ring, Aladdin is able to get the magic lamp back.

7. Gathering threads

The meaning in this novel is 'bringing together different things to make a conclusion', such as clues in a story, for example. The original meaning comes from making cloth. When you make a piece of cloth, you pull together lots of different threads to make a single piece of cloth.

◆ GLOSSARY ◆

airstrip COUNTABLE NOUN
An **airstrip** is a stretch of land
which has been cleared so that
aircraft can take off and land.

Aladdin PROPER NOUN
Aladdin is the main character in a
story about a poor young man
who obtains a magic lamp and
ring which can give him wishes.

alas ADVERB
You use **alas** to say that you think
that the facts you are talking
about are sad or unfortunate.

alibi COUNTABLE NOUN
If you have an **alibi**, you can
prove that you were somewhere
else when a crime was committed.

archaeologist COUNTABLE NOUN
An **archaeologist** studies
societies and peoples of the past
by examining the remains of their
buildings, tools, and other
objects.

as Allah wills PHRASE
As Allah wills is a translation of
the Arabic language expression
for "God willing", which means
you are saying that something will
happen if all goes well.

beloved ADJECTIVE
A **beloved** person, thing, or place
is one that you feel great
affection for.

blackmail UNCOUNTABLE NOUN
Blackmail is the action of
threatening to reveal a secret
about someone, unless they do
something you tell them to do,
such as giving you money.
TRANSITIVE VERB
If one person **blackmails** another
person, they use blackmail
against them.

boarding school VARIABLE NOUN
A **boarding school** is a school
which some or all of the pupils
live in during the school term.

brandy VARIABLE NOUN
Brandy is a strong alcoholic drink. It is often drunk after a meal.

brassière COUNTABLE NOUN
A **brassière** is the old-fashioned word for a bra.

break-in COUNTABLE NOUN
If there has been a **break-in**, someone has got into a building by force.

breathlessly ADVERB
If you do or say something **breathlessly**, you have difficulty in breathing properly, for example because you have been running or because you are afraid or excited.

buzzer COUNTABLE NOUN
A **buzzer** is an electrical device that is used to make a buzzing sound, for example to attract someone's attention.

catastrophe COUNTABLE NOUN
A **catastrophe** is an unexpected event that causes great suffering or damage.

colonel COUNTABLE NOUN
A **colonel** is a senior officer in an army, air force, or the marines.

consultation VARIABLE NOUN
A **consultation** with an expert is a meeting with them to discuss a particular problem and get their advice. **Consultation** is also the process of getting advice from an expert.

defence lawyer COUNTABLE NOUN
A **defence lawyer** is the lawyer who represents the defendant in court.

dice UNCOUNTABLE NOUN
Dice is a game which is played using dice. A **dice** is a small cube which has between one and six spots or numbers on its sides, and which is used in games to provide random numbers.

disapproval UNCOUNTABLE NOUN
If you feel or show **disapproval** of something or someone, you feel or show that you do not approve of them.

disgraceful ADJECTIVE
If you say that something such as behaviour or a situation is **disgraceful**, you feel that the person or people responsible should be ashamed of it.

drunken ADJECTIVE
A **drunken** person is drunk.

dryly ADVERB
If someone says something **dryly**, their voice is cold or dull, and does not express any emotions.

duchess COUNTABLE NOUN
A **duchess** is a woman who has the same rank as a duke, or who is a duke's wife or widow.

emir COUNTABLE NOUN
An **emir** is a Muslim ruler.

exclaim TRANSITIVE VERB
If someone **exclaims** something, they say it suddenly, loudly, or emphatically, often because they are excited, shocked, or angry.

fairy story COUNTABLE NOUN
A **fairy story** is a story for children involving magical events and imaginary creatures.

fingerprint COUNTABLE NOUN
Fingerprints are marks made by a person's fingers which show the lines on the skin. Everyone's fingerprints are different, so they can be used to identify criminals.

firmly ADVERB
If someone says something **firmly**, they say it in a way that shows that they are not going to change their mind, or that they are the person who is in control.

footstep COUNTABLE NOUN
A **footstep** is the sound that is made by someone walking when their foot touches the ground.

freckle COUNTABLE NOUN
Freckles are small light brown spots on someone's skin, especially on their face.

frown INTRANSITIVE VERB
When someone **frowns**, their eyebrows become drawn together, because they are annoyed, worried, or puzzled, or because they are thinking.

fuss INTRANSITIVE VERB
If you **fuss**, you worry or behave in a nervous, anxious way about unimportant matters or rush around doing unnecessary things.

gasp INTRANSITIVE VERB
When you **gasp**, you take a short quick breath through your mouth, especially when you are surprised, shocked, or in pain.

glare INTRANSITIVE VERB
If you **glare** at someone, you look at them with an angry expression on your face.

gloomily ADVERB
If someone says something **gloomily**, they sound like they are unhappy and have no hope.

godmother COUNTABLE NOUN
A young person's **godmother** is a woman who their parents have chosen to have a special relationship with them, and to help bring them up in the Christian religion.

grimly ADVERB
If someone says something **grimly**, they are very serious, usually because they are worried about something.

harmless ADJECTIVE
If you describe something as **harmless**, you mean that it is not important and therefore unlikely to annoy other people or cause trouble.

honour PASSIVE VERB
If you say that you **are honoured** by something, you are saying that you are grateful for it and pleased about it.

horrified TRANSITIVE VERB
If someone is **horrified**, they feel shocked or disgusted, usually because of something that they have seen or heard.

kneel INTRANSITIVE VERB
When you **kneel**, you bend your legs so that your knees are touching the ground.

lady TITLE NOUN
In Britain, **Lady** is a title used in front of the names of some female members of the nobility, or the wives of knights.

lawn VARIABLE NOUN
A **lawn** is an area of grass that is kept cut short and is usually part of someone's garden or backyard, or part of a park.

legacy COUNTABLE NOUN
A **legacy** is money or property which someone leaves to you when they die.

-like SUFFIX
-like is used after a noun to make an adjective that describes something as similar to or typical of the noun. For example 'business-like' means 'in an efficient or unemotional way, as you would do in business'.

likeness COUNTABLE NOUN
If you say that a picture of someone is a good **likeness**, you mean that it looks just like them.

locker COUNTABLE NOUN
A **locker** is a small metal or wooden cupboard with a lock, where you can put your personal possessions, for example in a school or sports club.

matron COUNTABLE NOUN
In boarding schools, the **matron** is the woman who looks after the health of the children.

mattress COUNTABLE NOUN
A **mattress** is the large, flat object which is put on a bed to make it comfortable to sleep on.

muscular ADJECTIVE
If a person or their body is **muscular**, they are very fit and strong, and have firm muscles which are not covered with a lot of fat.

my goodness EXCLAMATION
People sometimes say '**my goodness**' to express surprise.

nosey ADJECTIVE
If you describe someone as **nosey**, you mean that they are interested in things which do not concern them.

overhear TRANSITIVE VERB
If you **overhear** someone, you hear what they are saying when they are not talking to you and they do not know that you are listening.

pavilion COUNTABLE NOUN
A **pavilion** is a building on the edge of a sports field where players can change their clothes and wash.

persuasively ADVERB
If someone says something **persuasively**, they are likely to persuade a person to believe or do a particular thing.

physically ADVERB
If you talk about someone **physically**, you are talking about the qualities which are connected with their body, rather than with their mind.

pigeon COUNTABLE NOUN
A **pigeon** is a bird, usually grey in colour, which has a fat body. Pigeons often live in towns.

plain ADJECTIVE
If you describe someone as **plain**, you think they look ordinary and not at all beautiful.

Plasticine® UNCOUNTABLE NOUN
Plasticine® is a soft coloured substance like clay which children use for making models.

plump ADJECTIVE
You can describe someone or something as **plump** to indicate that they are rather fat or rounded.

prologue COUNTABLE NOUN
A **prologue** is a section of text that introduces a play or book.

ransom VARIABLE NOUN
A **ransom** is the money that has to be paid to someone so that they will set free a person they have kidnapped.

rebellion VARIABLE NOUN
A **rebellion** is a violent organized action by a large group of people who are trying to change their country's political system.

restring TRANSITIVE VERB
If you **restring** something such as a tennis racquet, you put new strings in it.

riddle COUNTABLE NOUN
You can describe something as a **riddle** if people have been trying to understand or explain it but have not been able to.

robe COUNTABLE NOUN
A **robe** is a loose piece of clothing which covers all of your body and reaches the ground. You can describe someone as wearing a robe or as wearing robes.

royalty UNCOUNTABLE NOUN
The members of royal families are sometimes referred to as **royalty**.

sabotage TRANSITIVE VERB
If a machine, railway line, or bridge is **sabotaged**, it is deliberately damaged or destroyed, for example in a war or as a protest.
UNCOUNTABLE NOUN
Sabotage is the act of sabotaging a machine, railway line, or bridge.

sandbag COUNTABLE NOUN
A **sandbag** is a cloth bag filled with sand. Sandbags are usually used to build walls for protection against floods or explosions.

settle in PHRASAL VERB
If you **settle in**, you become used to living in a new place, doing a new job, or going to a new school.

sharply ADVERB
If someone says something **sharply**, they say it suddenly and rather firmly or angrily, for example because they are warning or criticizing you.

sheikh COUNTABLE NOUN
A **sheikh** is a male Arab chief or ruler.

showdown UNCOUNTABLE NOUN
A **showdown** is a big argument or conflict which is intended to settle a dispute that has lasted for a long time.

sponge COUNTABLE NOUN
A **sponge** is a piece of a light, soft substance that you use for washing yourself or for cleaning things.

straw UNCOUNTABLE NOUN
Straw is the dried, yellow parts of crops such as wheat, used for animals to sleep on.

stumble INTRANSITIVE VERB
If you **stumble**, you put your foot down awkwardly while you are walking or running and nearly fall over.

sulkily ADVERB
If someone does or says something **sulkily**, they look or sound as if they are unwilling to enjoy themselves.

swap TRANSITIVE VERB
If you **swap** something with someone, you give it to them and receive a different thing in exchange. If you **swap** one thing for another, you remove the first thing and replace it with the second.

tap TRANSITIVE VERB
If someone **taps** your telephone, they attach a special device to the line so that they can secretly listen to your conversations.

thread COUNTABLE NOUN
The **thread** of an argument, a story, or a situation is an aspect of it that connects all the different parts together.

unofficially ADVERB
Something that is done **unofficially** is not organized or approved by a person or group in authority.

wig COUNTABLE NOUN
A **wig** is a covering of false hair which you wear on your head, for example because you have little hair of your own or because you want to cover up your own hair.

wreckage UNCOUNTABLE NOUN
When something such as a plane, car, or building has been destroyed, you can refer to what remains as **wreckage** or **the wreckage**.

COLLINS ENGLISH READERS ONLINE

Go online to discover the following useful resources for teachers and students:

- Downloadable audio of the story

- Classroom activities, including a plot synopsis

- Student activities, suitable for class use or for self-studying learners

- A level checker to ensure you are reading at the correct level

- Information on the Collins COBUILD Grading Scheme

All this and more at **www.collinselt.com/readers**

COLLINS ENGLISH READERS

Do you want to read more at your reading level? Try these:

AGATHA CHRISTIE MYSTERIES

Sparkling Cyanide 978-0-00-826234-1
Crooked House 978-0-00-826235-8
They Do It With Mirrors 978-0-00-826236-5
A Pocket Full of Rye 978-0-00-826237-2
Destination Unknown 978-0-00-826238-9
4.50 From Paddington 978-0-00-826239-6
Appointment with Death 978-0-00-826233-4
Peril at End House 978-0-00-826232-7
The Murder at the Vicarage 978-0-00-826231-0

Find out more at **www.collinselt.com/readers**